this one goes... I haven't read it yet :)
Love,
Grandma 12/25/20

Mystery of the Hidden Face

By the same author

MYSTERY OF THE PIRATE'S GHOST
MYSTERY OF THE SECRET MESSAGE
THE GREAT GOLD PIECE MYSTERY
MYSTERY OF THE WOODEN INDIAN
MYSTERY IN THE SQUARE TOWER
MYSTERY OF THE AUCTION TRUNK
MYSTERY AT THE DOLL HOSPITAL
MYSTERY OF THE DIAMOND NECKLACE

MYSTERY OF THE HIDDEN FACE

by Elizabeth Honness

Illustrated by Jacqueline Tomes

WILDSIDE PRESS

Copyright © 1963 by Elizabeth Honness

For my cousins

CYNTHIA LEIGH FORSYTHE
and MARIAN LEIGH OLEJER

who share in happy childhood memories of Clinton, New Jersey—the "Riverbend" of this story; and for their children: Jeffrey and Scott Forsythe—Kathie, Cynthia, Victoria, and Suzanne Leigh Olejer

The author wishes to express her gratitude to Mr. Theodor Siegl, Conservator of the Philadelphia Museum of Art and of the Pennsylvania Academy of Fine Arts, for his friendly advice and help with some of the technical details of this story, and also to Tracers Company of America for gracious permission to use its name.

Contents

I.	"A Dangerous Character"	13
II.	The Forgotten Fortune	21
III.	The Ancestor in the Attic	28
IV.	Vain Hope	40
V.	A Big Catch	49
VI.	Karl Hoffman	56
VII.	"Tidings of Joy"	64
VIII.	The Quarry	71
IX.	Another Rescue	80
X.	A Letter from Philadelphia	92
XI.	Something "Funny-Peculiar"	101
XII.	"Against My Will"	113
XIII.	The Art Thieves	121
XIV.	Karl Hoffman's Plan	129
XV.	Great-Grandmother's Secret	139
XVI.	Spilled Beans	147

Mystery of the Hidden Face

I

"A Dangerous Character"

The long June twilight was fading into dusk when the Lane family came home from their picnic on the river. A wash of gold still lingered on the horizon. Above, the sky deepened into nighttime blue and the evening star shone bright.

Debby, not quite three, yawned widely and sat down on the first porch step. "Debby sleepy," she said, rubbing two chubby fists at her eyes.

"Poor baby! It's way past your bedtime," said Jennifer, feeling grown-up and superior because she was eleven and was allowed to stay up until nine o'clock as a matter of course. Her short fair hair, tied into tassels

MYSTERY OF THE HIDDEN FACE

on each side of her head, bounced up and down as she took the steep porch steps two at a time. She unlatched the screen door and snapped on the hall light.

Debby held up her arms to Jeremy, who was twelve. "Ride Debby up steps," she commanded. Jerry bent willingly to his little sister and helped her clamber on, then piggy-backed her into the house. Mr. and Mrs. Lane followed with the picnic basket and thermos jugs.

"Jenny, you take Deb upstairs and start her bath. I'll be up as soon as I put these things in the kitchen," Mrs. Lane said. "Lend a hand, Jerry, will you? Your father wants to have a peaceful time with the evening paper."

Jenny and Debby started upstairs, but stopped short at a startled shout from the living room. "What the dickens has been going on here?" asked Mr. Lane. "Who turned over these chairs?"

Almost at once there was a sound of alarm from the kitchen, a low moan of distress from Mrs. Lane and an incredulous whistle from Jerry. "Jeepers, what a mess!" he shouted. "Hey, Dad, come quick!"

Jennifer grabbed Debby by the hand and raced for the kitchen. There she saw her mother, with Mr. Lane towering beside her, and Jeremy standing open-mouthed, gazing at the wreckage of the once tidy room. Pots and pans were scattered about, canned

"A DANGEROUS CHARACTER"

goods spilled over the floor. The vegetable bin was lying on its side, potatoes and carrots and onions strewn every which way. Torn fragments of newspaper, which had once lined the shelves storing canned foods, littered the linoleum. Coffee, flour, and sugar were poured on the kitchen counter from overturned canisters.

Debby began to cry. "Debby didn't do it, Debby didn't do it," she wailed.

Mr. Lane scooped her up in his arms. "Of course you didn't, darling. Don't cry." His lean, usually pleasant face became grim. "I'd like to catch the vandal who did, though."

Mrs. Lane looked as though she might cry too. "How will we ever get this mess cleaned up?"

Mr. Lane patted her shoulder. "It won't be so hard if we all pitch in and help."

"Do you s'pose it was a burglar?" asked Jennifer, feeling little creepy fingers of fear on her spine. "Maybe he's still in the house."

"A queer kind of burglar, if you ask me," said Jeremy. "Why should he want to make hash of our kitchen?"

"It's not only the kitchen," said Mr. Lane, putting down Debby who had now stopped crying. "The living room hasn't been spared either, though it's nothing as bad as this. We'd better look over the rest of the house. Mother and I'll go first. Here, Dorothy," he said, handing Mrs. Lane a broom. "I'll get a poker from the fireplace and we'll be armed at least."

Jenny and Jerry took their places on either side of Debby and she slipped her soft little hand into theirs. Each felt safer with this warm contact as they followed their parents on a tour of the house.

The dining room seemed untouched except for a pair of candlesticks knocked over on the sideboard. In the living room, as their father had said, several straight chairs had been upset, sofa pillows were on the floor, and a standing lamp had fallen across a big wing chair.

Mr. Lane picked up the fireplace poker and led the way into the hall. They saw that the double doors into the parlor were closed. Maybe the burglar was hiding in there! Jennifer's heart thumped as her dad pressed the light switch and slid open the doors. No one was there. The polished rosewood of the baby-grand piano shone serenely in the light, the Victorian chairs and sofas and marble-top tables were in their usual places, just as they had been arranged in great-grandmother's day. Nothing had been touched.

Mr. Lane closed the double doors. He headed for the stairs. Mrs. Lane followed close behind, her broom gripped so hard her knuckles showed white.

We do look funny, Jennifer thought, eying her

"A DANGEROUS CHARACTER"

father's tall figure, poker in hand, with small, dainty mother at his heels, carrying the broom. She suppressed a giggle.

Debby hung back. "No want to go," she whispered.

"Don't be afraid, Deb. Dad won't let anything happen to us," Jerry told her. "Come on now, let's catch up to them."

They moved quietly up the stairs, along the upper hall, and into the doorway of their parents' room. Light flooded the room as Mr. Lane touched the switch. "Well!" he said. "Well! Will you look what we have here!"

"I'll be dog-goned!" said Jeremy. "A raccoon!"

Sitting in the middle of the bedroom rug was a gray furry animal about three feet long, with a bushy tail ringed round and round with stripes of black. He

was holding a cantaloupe in his little black hands, chewing it busily, not in the least concerned at having been exposed as the intruder.

Jennifer began to laugh. "Oh me, oh my!" she sputtered. "What a funny burglar!"

Mother set down her broom and leaned beside it against the wall. She began to laugh too. Jeremy and Debby joined in, and soon the whole family was weak with laughter. The raccoon kept his black eyes fixed on them, but continued feeding.

"Henry, you do look so funny with that poker," gasped Mrs. Lane. "All set to do battle with a dangerous character! How are we going to get him out of here?"

"Look, he's wearing a mask and black kid gloves just the way a burglar should!" said Jerry.

The markings of black fur across his eyes did look like a mask and his little forepaws, which held the melon, were leathery and black.

"See how daintily he eats," said Mrs. Lane.

Mr. Lane propped his poker against a chair and walked slowly to one of the twin beds. "You won't like this, Dorothy," he said to Mrs. Lane, "but it's the only way I can think to catch him." He twitched the bedspread from the bed and dropped it over the raccoon. The animal gave a squeal of rage.

"Help me wrap him up in it, Jerry," Mr. Lane

"A DANGEROUS CHARACTER"

said. The bedspread was wriggling and moving as the raccoon struggled to get free. A series of twittering sounds ending in a piercing bleat came from within the spread as the raccoon realized he was trapped.

Jerry and his father swathed the spread around the animal. They slid a portion of it under him and lifted him off the floor, holding him as though he were in a sack.

"Can we keep him? Can we keep him?" asked Jennifer, bobbing up and down, her tassels waving.

"All I want is for you to get him out of here," said Mrs. Lane, wiping tears of laughter from her eyes. "Put him in the old chicken run for tonight. We can decide what to do with him tomorrow."

Mr. Lane and Jeremy carried their bundle as far away from their legs as they could to prevent the raccoon's sharp claws from reaching them through the bedspread.

"Bye-bye," said Debby. "Raccoon go bed. Debby go bed too."

Jennifer stooped before her. "Climb on, Deb. I'll ride you to bed."

"It's so late we'll skip your bath tonight," said Mother.

Debby's warm arms clasped Jenny's neck and her head nestled into its nape as Jenny jogged across the hall to Debby's room. "Here we are!" She straightened up beside Debby's crib, facing away from it, and jogged up and down until Debby's arms let go and she landed on the mattress with a bounce, her soft hair flying. "Do it again!" she pleaded. "One more time. Please!"

"Not any more tonight," Jennifer said firmly as she handed Debby her nightie. She bent down and kissed Debby's smooth pink cheek. "You go sleepy-by now. Get undressed and into your nightie. Mommy will be along to tuck you in. I'm going to fill a pan of water for Mr. Raccoon so he can have a drink in case he gets thirsty in the night."

II

The Forgotten Fortune

When Mr. Lane and Jennifer and Jerry returned from settling the raccoon in his new home, Mrs. Lane was ready to begin the clean-up job in the kitchen.

"Dad says we may keep him, if you're willing," said Jennifer. "He seems to like his new home. And he was very grateful for the water." She looked at her mother anxiously.

"As long as you keep him out of here, I suppose he's welcome," said Mother.

Jennifer gave her mother a quick hug.

"He must have climbed in this window we left open," said Mr. Lane, indicating the one over the sink. "Look, he pushed the screen out."

Mrs. Lane looked around the kitchen. "Who would ever think one medium-sized animal could create such havoc! I guess the first thing to do is to clean up the counter, then pick up the pots and pans and sweep the floor."

She assigned the work. "Jerry, run down to the basement and bring up some newspapers from the pile there. Then you and Jenny can fold them into new shelf papers and stow the cans away in the cupboard. Please keep the soups together and put the meats and vegetables and tuna fish on the lower shelves. Henry, will you put the pots and pans away while I try to rescue some of this flour and sugar and coffee and get them back into the canisters?"

Mr. Lane hung the saucepans on their hooks below the shelves that held Mrs. Lane's cookbooks. The shiny metal pans knocked out a sort of tune as they touched each other swinging from their hooks. "I read somewhere that raccoons like bright and shiny things," said Mr. Lane. "I suppose these pans were irresistible."

Jennifer gathered up potatoes and onions and carrots and put them back in the vegetable bin. She finished just as Jeremy arrived with a stack of newspapers and they began to fold them lengthwise the width of the storage closet shelves. As they worked, Jerry's glance fell on a headline in one paper.

"What are lost hairs?" he asked.

"Lost hares? I can't imagine," said Mrs. Lane. "Did someone lose his pet rabbits perhaps? Read the rest of the story."

Jerry read, " 'Forgotten Fortunes. Windfalls await lost hairs.' "

Mr. Lane hid a smile. "That word is spelled h e i r, isn't it? The h is silent; it's pronounced 'air.' It means someone who will inherit money or property. What are you reading, anyhow?"

"*The Philadelphia Inquirer*," said Jerry. "Here's what it says:

> "THE INQUIRER as a public service in cooperation with Tracers Company of America, a New York investigating firm, is aiding in the search for scores of persons entitled to various sums in 'forgotten fortunes.'
>
> "The money is in stock dividends accumulated from securities once believed to have been worthless. The sums range from a few dollars to thousands."

"Wheee! wouldn't it be cool if we were one of those persons!" burst out Jenny. "Go on, read some more."

Jerry continued: " 'Tracers Company estimates that thirty per cent of the original holders are deceased'—what does that mean?"

"Dead," said his father.

" 'In these cases their *h*eirs'—I mean *airs*—'or next of kin are entitled to the assets. Periodically Tracers Company draws up a list of names of persons entitled to the money. The list, giving last-known addresses, is published every Friday in THE INQUIRER.' Gee, there's quite a list of them!"

"Look and see if we are there," Jenny urged.

Jerry glanced down the column of names. "I don't see any Lanes listed in Philadelphia or New Jersey," he said. "Hey, wait a minute! Your middle name is Calvert, Dad. There's a Calvert—Robert Bancroft Calvert. 'Last known address: Princeton, New Jersey.' Could he be any kin of yours?"

"Not likely," said Mr. Lane. "Calvert is a common enough name. I suspect there are lots of them who aren't related to us."

"It might be worth looking up some family history," said Mrs. Lane. "Wouldn't it be fun if we discovered he *was* related—a distant cousin or something —and that we are his only next of kin!"

They had stopped work while Jerry read. Mr. Lane had been dipping into the cookie jar. He wiped crumbs from his mouth and grinned at his wife teasingly. "I see you are building air castles already— dreaming up a fabulous fortune, ours for the asking!

Even in the remote chance that we are related, like as not there would be other relatives closer than ourselves."

Jenny's face fell. "Don't you know anything about the Calverts?" she asked.

"I know I was named for my great-grandfather," said Mr. Lane. "There was some sort of story in the family that he had been adopted by his Uncle Charles when he was a small baby, after his mother died. Her name was Melissa and she was married to a Calvert. The little boy's real name was Henry Lane Calvert, but when he came to live with his Uncle Charles the last two names were switched around so he would have Lane for a last name like the rest of the family."

"Well," said Mother, "it certainly can't hurt to look up the genealogy and to ask that Tracers Company to give you some further information." She glanced at the kitchen clock. "It's getting late. Let's hurry and finish cleaning up."

Jennifer thought about the family as she worked. All that Dad had told them seemed so far away in the past. She knew his father and mother had been killed in a train accident when he was only six and that he had been brought up by his Grandfather and Grandmother Lane in this very house. They were her and Jerry's great-grandparents, of course. She remembered them. Great-Grandfather had not been well for a long time before he died and she and Jerry always had to be quiet and not run and shout when they came to visit him. He was very old, with thin white hair and cheeks that were puckered all over with tiny wrinkles. He smelled of witch hazel. If she screwed her eyes tight shut she could see Great-Grandmother, a spry little birdlike lady hurrying to wait on him. She had always been glad to see Jerry and Jenny and kept a supply of cookies and peppermints for them.

When both great-grandparents had died four years ago, within a few months of each other, it had not touched her very deeply. Daddy, as their only grandchild, had inherited a little money and this house. The Lanes had moved here from a rented house on the other side of town.

The kitchen did not look at all the way it had when Daddy was a boy. One of the first things Mother insisted on having made over was the kitchen. A big bay window had been built out of one wall. It had little square panes of glass and a sill wide enough to hold pots of red geraniums and the chives and herbs. Now there were plenty of cupboards of knotty pine and a wall oven with a window so you could look in at what was happening. Great-Grandma's black Boston rocker was still here. Debby loved to rock in it, either on Mother's lap, or alone, when, crooning little songs, she made the chair travel all over the kitchen.

Jenny could hear her dad putting things straight in the living room. She set the last can of soup in place and stepped out of her mother's way as she swept the torn papers into a dustpan.

"Thanks for helping, honey," said Mrs. Lane. "And you, too, Son. I've been won over to keeping the raccoon. If it hadn't been for him, we might never have known about the chance of Dad's being a missing heir!"

III

The Ancestor in the Attic

The first whistle of the cardinal outside his window awoke Jerry next morning. It seemed to call *hurry, hurry, hurry* over and over with a gurgling *chug-chug-chug—chug-chug* in between. He jumped into his clothes and poked his head into Jenny's room. Seeing she was asleep, he softly closed the door, an act of unusual consideration.

Debby was sliding over the side of her crib as he reached her room at the head of the stairs. Her face was flushed with sleep, her corn-silk hair curling about her cheeks.

"Do you want to go with me to feed the raccoon?"

THE ANCESTOR IN THE ATTIC

he asked. "Put on some clothes and I'll help you tie your shoes."

"Debby go wash first," said Debby.

When she came back, she climbed into a pair of shorts and pulled a jersey over her head. Jerry helped her lace her sneakers and together they tiptoed downstairs. He filled a pitcher with water and opened a can of sardines. "Raccoons eat fish," he told Debby. "I hope ours likes this kind."

She babbled happily at his side as they went out the kitchen door and approached the old henhouse in the back yard.

The Lane house was built on the slope of Quarry Hill, so called for the lime quarry and kilns which had been operated in Riverbend long ago. There was a level lawn in front of the house, bordered by a heavy wire fence made of overlapping loops of wire painted white. The front walk of bricks, set on edge in herringbone pattern, was reached through a gate in the fence. The lawn continued up a rather steep bank at the side, where it leveled out again to the depth of the house. Just beyond the grape arbor it sloped upward with increasing steepness to the crown of Quarry Hill. Hollyhocks, just beginning to bloom, marched up this incline.

Directly at the rear of the house was a slanting garden patch where Mr. Lane grew lettuce, radishes, tomatoes, peas, beans, and a row or two of sweet corn, as his grandfather had before him. A two-foot-high concrete wall kept the garden soil from washing down against the house during heavy rains. Behind this wall was the narrow chicken coop with a runway enclosed in wire. The coop itself now held Mr. Lane's gardening tools. The raccoon was clinging to the wire netting, peering out between his two black paws, his black nose poked through a hole in the wire.

Debby danced up and down when she saw him.

"Don't pat him," cautioned Jerry. "He might bite. He looks as though he were waiting for us to come. As soon as we feed him I am going to find a big branch to put in there so he will have something else to climb on."

The raccoon dropped down from the netting and backed into a corner near the chicken coop, watching Jerry's every movement. Jerry quickly poured water into a pan and put the saucer of sardines down before it, then stepped out, fastening the door after him.

"What raccoon's name? What his name?" sang Debby as the raccoon approached the sardines, sniffed at them delicately, then picked up one in his little black-gloved paws. He dipped the small fish into the water, washed it carefully, then began to eat it with greedy satisfaction.

"He hasn't a name. You name him," said Jerry.

THE ANCESTOR IN THE ATTIC

Debby puckered her forehead. Her face cleared. She clapped her hands together. "He named Racky-Pooh," she declared. "Pooh for Pooh Bear, and Racky 'cause he's a raccoon."

"That's a good name," said Jerry. "It suits him."

Birds were making happy sounds in the trees and the sweetness of honeysuckle and lilacs came to the children from beyond the garden. It was going to be hot later on, but the June sun was now only pleasantly warm.

Jerry and Debby climbed through dewy grass to the end of the yard, where Jerry found a big branch that had blown off a maple tree during a storm. He and Debby dragged it back to the hen yard. Jerry pulled it inside and propped it against the wire netting, bending the leafy top where it was too tall. The leaves spread out against the wire ceiling, making an area of shade.

"Now Racky-Pooh will be more contented with a tree to climb," said Jerry. "Let's go back to the kitchen and get out all the fixings for pancakes." Sunday pancakes were a tradition in the Lane family. The first person up was expected to set the table and lay out the ingredients so that when Mrs. Lane came down everything would be ready for mixing.

After Sunday school and church, while Mrs. Lane

was putting the finishing touches on dinner, Mr. Lane took down the family Bible from the secretary desk in the living room. It was a very large, heavy volume, bound in brown leather that had been preserved through the years by frequent rubbing with saddle soap. Mr. Lane cleared magazines and books from the end of a drop-leaf table and laid the Bible on it. Then he opened to some pages in the center, between the Old and New Testaments, that were provided for the listings of births and marriages and deaths in the family.

Jenny and Jerry were not allowed to touch the Bible, it was so very old and special. But they liked to look at these pages filled with so many different kinds of handwriting. Some writing was cramped and tight. Other entries were written in what their dad called copperplate—beautiful and neat and graceful, with the broad strokes of the pen changing into delicate thin lines, then finishing off with curlicues and flourishes —nothing like the kind of printing-writing Jenny and Jerry had been taught in school.

There were entries going back long before the early seventeen hundreds when the first Lane had come from England and brought this Bible with him. His forebears, his children, and his children's children were listed in faded script. Mr. Lane turned the page and hunted until he found the name of Phoebe King

Lane, born in 1782. "That was the year after General George Washington defeated Lord Cornwallis at the battle of Yorktown," said Mr. Lane. "She lived to be ninety-four—a great old age."

Phoebe King Lane's portrait hung in the dining room over the chest where Mother kept table linens.

Jenny could see her now through the wide double doorway. She was a severe-looking old lady in a fluted lace bonnet with a wide white pleated shawl collar crisscrossed over her bosom. She sat erect, with her hands folded in her lap, the polished back of the straight chair just visible behind one shoulder.

Her eyes were what one noticed first. Pale blue and penetrating behind steel-rimmed glasses, they looked right at you. No matter where Jenny sat or stood in view of the portrait, her great-great-great-great-grandmother's eyes sought her out. Jenny was sure the old lady could tell when she had been naughty. At the dining table Jerry insisted on sitting in the chair that let him keep his back to the portrait so the old lady could not look disapproving when he forgot his table manners.

Jenny remembered the first time they had seen the painting. It was the day they had moved into Great-Grandfather's house, when she had been seven. Debby had not been born until the following summer.

It was exciting to move. Jerry and she had raced up and down stairs, exploring the house that looked so different with half-empty rooms and no old people to be quiet for. They had gotten in everyone's way until finally, in desperation, Mother had told them to either go outdoors or up to the attic to play.

The attic had been their choice. It was there they

THE ANCESTOR IN THE ATTIC

had found the portrait, face to the eaves, leaning against the tilt of the roof. They had dragged it out into the dim light and used an old rag to dust off the wide mahogany frame.

Mrs. Lane had been delighted with their find. "Imagine discovering an ancestor in the attic!" she had exclaimed. "Henry, who was she? Do you have any idea?"

Mr. Lane had looked at the portrait of the severe old lady for a long time before speaking. "She's my great-great-great-grandmother," he said at last. "I remember finding her up here once myself when I was only a year or so younger than Jeremy. I asked my grandfather who she was and he told me. She was his great-grandmother, Phoebe King Lane. He didn't feel too kindly toward her, he wouldn't tell me why. Said the dark attic was a good enough place for her. He didn't want her downstairs on his wall where she would be watching him all the time and looking down her nose at everything he did."

"Well," Mrs. Lane had said. "I don't care if he didn't like her. I do! She has a strong wonderful old face. She may have been hard to live with when she was alive, but that shouldn't bother any of us now. She'll look handsome above that mahogany chest in the dining room."

And so she did, even though there was a slight crack

in the board on which the picture was painted and places where the paint had flaked off. Friends who came to call on the Lanes admired the portrait and Mrs. Lane never tired of telling how Jenny and Jerry had discovered their ancestor in the attic. As for those two, they had a hard time remembering the number of "greats" she was to them. Four, their mother said, but that was too many to say, one after another, so they just called her four-times-Great-Grandma.

The entry in the Bible indicated that Phoebe King was the daughter of Jonathan and Mary King. Her dates were 1782–1876. She had been married to Henry Griswald Lane in 1800. Listed below were the names of their children: James, Henry, Cynthia, Deborah, David, Charles, Lucinda, and Melissa—eight in all.

"They sure had big families in those days," said Jeremy.

"Yes," said Mr. Lane, "but note the dates beside their names. You'll see that a number of them didn't live very long. They died when they were babies or just a few years old. James lived only a year. Cynthia was ten when she died, Deborah two, and Lucinda four."

Jenny looked shocked. "Why?" she asked. She remembered tiny marble headstones in the family plot

THE ANCESTOR IN THE ATTIC

in the Riverbend cemetery and could imagine all of the tears that had been wept over them. "Why did they have to die when they were so young?"

"Chiefly because the medical discoveries that we take for granted now hadn't been made then," said her father. "There was no penicillin, for instance. No shots for diphtheria, whooping cough, polio, or typhoid fever. Lots of children, and grown-ups, too, caught those and died. Not as much was known about the importance of good sanitation, either, or pure water and milk and sewage disposal. Things like that."

Jenny remembered how Debby squealed when the doctor had to stick her with a needle. She supposed she had squealed herself when she was that young. Now she was brave about injections. But she appreciated in a new way how lucky she was to be living today when children were protected from those diseases. Poor Phoebe King—to have lost four children, three of them when they were babies. She must have felt very sad and bitter at times. Maybe that was why her face had lines and looked so stern.

Mr. Lane pointed to the name "Melissa"—last born of Phoebe's children. "I believe she was my great-great-grandmother," he said. "She only lived a short while after her son was born." Beside her name were the dates 1822–1842. She had married Bancroft Calvert in 1839 and had one son, Henry Lane Calvert, born in 1841. Then a year later, at the age of twenty, she had died.

"Now we're getting somewhere!" exclaimed Jerry. "Calvert! That's the name we want."

"Yes, that's it," said Mr. Lane. "Henry Lane Calvert, Melissa's baby, was adopted by her brother Charles." He read out of the Bible the name Charles King Lane, born 1810, died 1895, married to Amanda Carhart in 1835, and the list of his children, which included Henry Calvert Lane with his dates. There was nothing to indicate that he was the child of Melissa and that he had been christened Henry Lane Calvert.

"I'm afraid any hard-headed banker who was custodian of the forgotten fortune of Robert Bancroft Calvert would insist on more proof than this that I am descended from Bancroft Calvert," said Mr. Lane.

Jenny had been studying the page of names in deep concentration, thinking of all these old people whose blood ran in her veins. It made her feel queer, as though she were not really herself but a jumble, a mixture of the many people who had gone before. All at once something odd about the entry for Melissa caught her attention. "Look!" she said. "Why do you suppose somebody drew a line through Melissa's name?"

Jerry peered at the faded script. Sure enough, a line had been firmly drawn through that one name.

THE ANCESTOR IN THE ATTIC

"I don't know the answer," said their father. "It is something I have wondered about for a long time."

At that moment Mrs. Lane appeared at the dining room doorway. "Dinner is ready," she said.

IV

Vain Hope

The next day, Monday, the sky was slate-gray and rain fell heavily, running in rivulets down the side of Quarry Hill, pouring out onto the side lawn, making furrows of water through Mr. Lane's vegetable garden. Racky-Pooh curled himself into a ball in the crotch of the maple branch and let the water slide off his fur.

There was nothing for the children to do but stay indoors, hold long telephone conversations with their friends, read, and play games. Debby blew soap bubbles in the kitchen, slopped about with finger paints, and talked to her teddy bear. Their mother made

VAIN HOPE

cookies and a cake. The three licked the beater and bowls.

Late in the afternoon when the rain slackened, Jenny and Jerry put on high boots, yellow slickers, and rain hats and walked overtown. They passed the long white-verandahed Riverbend House, noted for its good food, and walked on top of the stone wall bordering the sidewalk that led to the bridge. From this height they could see the hurrying brown waters of the river. They crossed to the far side of the bridge and leaned on the railing to watch the water pour over the dam in a smooth brown flood which turned into a mass of foam as it hit the dam apron, then rushed along over rocks. Jerry tossed a stick over the rail and saw the water seize it and send it tumbling onward.

Town traffic still used this old iron-and-wood bridge. It rattled and rumbled like thunder when cars crossed over its plank floor. There was a newer concrete bridge downstream that carried the four-lane highway around the town, but one time this had been the only bridge over the river on the main road from New York City to the West. It had a walkway at each side, protected by the high bridge trusses from the traffic in the center, where two modern cars barely had room to pass.

"Golly, the river's high!" said Jerry. He had to shout to make Jenny hear, the water made such a roar pouring over the dam.

Jenny nodded. She hoped, now the rain had nearly stopped, tomorrow would be a nice day. Jerry had promised to take her with him fishing, since Tom Jordan, his best friend, was away visiting at the shore. Tom's sister Frannie was with him, alas, which meant that she, Jennie, was without her bosom pal, too. Tom and Frannie would come home brown as berries and the four of them would have fun together. Meanwhile she and Jerry had to make do with each other.

VAIN HOPE

Tomorrow, for sure, if they did go fishing, they would have to bail out the boat. It was tied up to a dock above the old mill where Spruce Run flowed into the river.

She tried to imagine what Riverbend had been like when the first settlers built the dam and the two mills on either side. The stone one had been used to grind grain for flour in the old days, the red wooden one was a talc mill. They had both been idle for years. Recently the talc mill had been converted into the Riverbend Art Center, where local artists could show their work and where classes were held for people who wanted to learn to paint. Mother was one of them. She went to a class once a week when Martha came to clean and Grandmother Turner took care of Debby. It was fun for Mother. She always came home from class bubbling with enthusiasm and wishing time could be stretched so she wouldn't have to stop work on a painting. The only thing she didn't enjoy was washing the dirty paintbrushes afterward.

Mr. Hoffman, the art teacher, lived in the mill. He had come to Riverbend a year ago as a refugee from East Germany. A small apartment had been fitted up for him on the top floor of the mill where he lived rent-free, and he was paid a modest wage for managing the art center. He told Mother he earned enough from his art classes and the occasional sales he made of his own work to get along quite well.

Jenny had seen him only from a distance. He kept to himself, though he was friendly enough, people said. He had very blond hair and he wore old jeans and a striped jersey. You could guess he was an artist straight off. She wondered how he liked the roar of the waterfall day and night, though of course most of the time it didn't make as much noise as now. The mill must be a nice place to live, with the craggy heights of Quarry Hill towering over it and the smooth river with weeping willows trailing their fingers in the water and the constant gurgling sound when the river was peaceful.

No wonder artists liked Riverbend, she thought. The mills were so like a picture with their raceways and waterfall. Above the dam, where the river branched, there was a marshy meadow bordered by water lilies and filled with marsh marigolds and creamy-white and pink mallow flowers. The river looped its way through town, where the marshy meadows gave way to neat back yards, which sloped down to the water. Along the river bank were docks with rowboats tied up to them. The houses, which were situated on higher, sloping ground, had three stories in the rear, and just two in front. There was an uptown bridge as well as this one; and down Leigh Street, where Grandmother Turner lived, there was

VAIN HOPE

still another bridge over Beaver Brook, which rippled between narrow banks along the back yards until it turned south and joined the river below the highway bridge. People sometimes called Riverbend a little Venice because there was so much water around.

There certainly was water around now! It was overflowing the gutters on Main Street and slopping over the sidewalks in front of the stores. Jenny and Jerry left the bridge and splashed happily through the flood, sending eddies and curls of water whirling out from their boots.

"Good day for ducks!" called Mr. Pardee from the door of his dry-goods store. "Lucky it's stopping or the water would be rolling in my front door." Jenny and Jerry had often heard tales of high water in the past when the stores along Main Street had been flooded.

The rain really seemed to have stopped. Jenny looked up. The mass of gray clouds overhead had broken apart and were beginning to move across the sky. She pointed upward. "Almost enough blue to make a Dutchman a pair of breeches," she said. "That means fair weather. See!"

"I see something better," said Jerry. "Here comes Dad!"

The three of them sloshed home together through the puddles.

MYSTERY OF THE HIDDEN FACE

At supper Mr. Lane told them he had written Tracers Company of America, asking for information about Robert Bancroft Calvert. "I said in the letter that I believed I was descended from a Bancroft Calvert who had married my great-great-grandmother, Melissa Lane, but I didn't give any details or mention the adoption of her baby by her brother. I expect the next step will be for them to put me in touch with the custodian of the Calvert estate and then will come the matter of proofs, which we don't have. Chances are there is some descendant who is closer than I, even if I could prove I am who I am. So don't get your hopes up, kids and don't do any talking about this outside the family."

"How could there be anybody closer?" demanded Jenny indignantly.

"Well, suppose Bancroft Calvert married again after Melissa died and had other children and they had children and so on. The ones living today would have as much claim as I."

Mrs. Lane got up to clear the table. "I know, in my right mind, it is only a pipe dream," she said, laughing. "Things like forgotten fortunes suddenly falling into one's lap don't happen often in real life. At least, not very often! We don't even know whether our Bancroft Calvert is related to this Robert Bancroft Calvert who died in Princeton."

VAIN HOPE

"True," said Dad as he untied Debby's bib. "At least they each have 'Bancroft' as a given name. That's something to go on."

"Unless," said Mother, pausing in the doorway and continuing her own train of thought, "unless there is some written record lying around that we haven't discovered. It seems odd to me that you would have been told your great-grandfather was Melissa's son and that he was adopted by his Uncle Charles and we can't find anything in writing to prove it."

Jenny gathered up a load of dishes and followed her mother. "Do you s'pose there might be some papers hidden somewhere?" she asked. She felt excited inside. Maybe she and Jerry could find some long-missing documents which would prove beyond question Dad's right to the lost fortune.

Mrs. Lane smiled ruefully as she began to scrape the dishes before putting them into the dishwasher. "Dad is perfectly right to tell us not to get our hopes up," she said. "If this were a story someone was writing, it would be so easy to have the heroine, a girl just your age, find a journal tucked away in a secret drawer in an old desk, and there would be all the proof she needed."

"You read my mind, Mommy. That is just what I was thinking."

"But our old desk doesn't have a secret drawer,"

MYSTERY OF THE HIDDEN FACE

said Mrs. Lane. "Your father and I went through all the family papers and letters we inherited with this house. There wasn't a single letter or will or diary that mentioned in any way that his Great-Grandfather Henry Calvert Lane had been adopted and had had his last name changed from Calvert to Lane. It is just a story handed down in the family by word of mouth, so we'd better not waste any time in vain hopes. I'm telling this to myself as much as to you, dear."

Jenny turned away without answering. Mommy might feel that way, but she didn't have to. That was the trouble with grown-ups. They always insisted on bringing you down to earth. As she pushed open the swinging door to the dining room her eyes met the eyes of Phoebe King Lane looking through her steel-rimmed spectacles in the portrait. "You know a secret," Jenny said to her under her breath. "I wish I could figure out a way to make you tell it!"

V

A Big Catch

"*Oh what a beautiful morning; Oh what a beautiful day!*" sang Jenny, doing a dance step to keep up with Jeremy. The wickerwork creel bounced on her back and she rattled two bailing cans together like castanets. Jerry strode ahead, fishing rods over his shoulder.

Too bad Tom was away and couldn't go fishing, she thought, but good luck for her! Jerry would never have let her come along otherwise.

It was indeed a sparkling day, new-washed and clean after yesterday's rain. The leaves seemed lacquered with sunshine, shimmering and moving constantly in a green dance, tossing and turning in the sunlit air. The sound of the waterfall—not as loud as yesterday—came to them as they left Main Street at the bridge and passed by the entrance to the quarry with its open lime kilns. They turned into the lane which led past the Riverbend Art Center. Presently they came to where their boat was tied up.

A light breeze was sending ripples racing each other on the surface of the river. It lifted Jenny's bangs from her forehead. The long reeds and grasses in the meadow across the river waved and bowed as the wind swept over them.

Jerry and Jenny bailed the boat energetically with the two large tomato juice cans, which were dented at the lips to form V's. This made it easier to scoop water from the corners of the flat-bottomed boat. Finally the last canful was tossed over the side.

Jerry handed Jenny the fish poles and his tin of worms which he had dug early that morning in the garden. Then he untied the rope from the ring in the dock, stepped aboard, and pushed off with one oar. The boat tilted with his weight. Jenny shifted herself on the wide stern seat to keep the boat balanced. Jerry adjusted the oars in the oarlocks and with steady strokes rowed into midstream and headed up Spruce Run. The river was still high, but nothing like the way it had been the day before.

An emerald dragonfly flashed close to Jenny's head,

A BIG CATCH

making her duck. Water bugs scurried away, skating swiftly on the water. Jenny pushed her finger about in the can of worms, bringing a fat wriggling one to the surface. With gritted teeth she threaded it on the hook of Jerry's line, then repeated this brave act for her own fish hook. "Ugh!" she said, wiping her fingers on her shorts.

"Why are girls so sissy about worms?" asked Jerry.

"They're so slimy and they feel so horrid to the touch! But I said I'd bait the hooks if you took me fishing, and I did it!" Jenny was unable to conceal her pride. "Don't ask me to pretend I like it, though!"

MYSTERY OF THE HIDDEN FACE

The fish were biting. Jenny felt a tug on her line almost as soon as the hook sank into the water. The bright orange bobber tied to her line several inches above the hook floated serenely one moment. The next it began to move in quick jerks as the fish took the worm and discovered he had a hook as well in his mouth. "A bite! A bite!" shouted Jenny. She stood up and tugged so hard the fish flashed out of the water and soared overhead to land with a splash on the far side of the boat.

"That's not the way to do it!" said Jerry. "You've got to pull a fish in slow and easy. Don't be in such a blasted hurry!"

Jenny tried again. This time she managed to land the fish inside the boat. It was a sunfish of good size and it flopped and floundered at the end of the line, its eyes staring, mouth gasping.

"Not bad," said Jerry. "You're lucky it didn't come off the hook when it sailed over the boat." She felt very proud as Jerry slipped the fish into the slot in the creel, and silently grateful that he hadn't made her take it off the hook.

He shipped the oars and allowed the boat to drift gently with the current, which was sluggish here where the water was backed up so far behind the dam. They fished in silence, punctuated with squeals from Jennifer whenever she felt a tug on her line.

A BIG CATCH

Jerry had luck, too. His most exciting catch was a pickerel, a big fellow fully eighteen inches long. Jerry played him, letting him run with the bait. The reel sang as the fish darted as far as the line would allow him to go. Then Jerry reeled him in patiently, closer and closer to the boat after each run, until the fish was exhausted and Jerry triumphantly lifted him out of the water.

"Phew!" he whistled. "He was a fighter all right! And big enough to have for supper."

"If we piece out with some of my sunnies," said Jenny. "I'm going to be hungry! Won't Racky-Pooh be glad we caught so many!"

She gazed at the fish admiringly. "He's a whopper!"

They had been so intent on landing the big fish, admiring him, and removing the hook from his mouth, they had not noticed how far the river had been carrying them. Suddenly the sound of the water flowing over the dam was loud in their ears. Jenny looked up startled. Their boat was perilously close to the crest of the dam and moving faster.

"Jerry!" she cried. "Back water quick or we'll go over!"

Jerry had his back to the falls. He grabbed the oars and tried to push the boat stern-first against the current. As soon as he lifted the oars to take another stroke, the rush of the river carried them forward

MYSTERY OF THE HIDDEN FACE

again. Jenny sat frozen with fright as they swept closer and closer to the brink.

"Here, look sharp! Catch this rope!" someone shouted. The voice came from the mill. Jenny saw Mr. Hoffman, the artist, leaning from a window of the art center. He hurled one end of a rope, knotted around a hammer, through the air. It landed in the boat with a thud and Jerry pounced on it and held on. The boat jerked to a halt just short of the falls.

The freckles stood out sharply on Jenny's white face as she realized how near they had come to going over. She shuddered.

"Hold on tight," called Mr. Hoffman. "I'll haul you in."

Slowly but steadily their rowboat slid toward the mill where the artist, framed by the window, pulled the rope hand over hand.

"He's reeling us in just like a fish," said Jenny, beginning to feel safe again and to enjoy the excitement.

When the prow of the boat finally nudged the wall of the mill, Mr. Hoffman leaned out of the window toward them. His eyes were intensely blue. "A good thing I looked up from my work just then! It is not safe in a boat to become so absorbed that you do not see where you are going." He spoke very good English with a slight accent.

A BIG CATCH

"Gee, we sure thank you!" said Jerry, his voice shaking. "What do we do now?"

"I suggest that the little girl—your sister, is she not?—move up into the prow of the boat and take hold of that ring in the wall. Then she can push the boat along the wall, you helping with one oar, until you get round the end of the wall and float into the millrace. The gates are closed, so there is no current there. Once out of the current, you can row, keeping close to the bank, until you come to where you tie up the boat."

"I don't know how we'll ever thank you," said Jenny.

"Stop in and visit me on your way home," said the artist. "I should like to see how big are the fish you have caught. Oh, and I'd like to have my hammer back, if you do not object." He smiled, showing even white teeth.

Jerry had been hanging on to his end of the rope with the hammer. He let go and Mr. Hoffman pulled it up to his window.

VI

Karl Hoffman

A handsomely lettered sign above the door of the old mill identified it as the RIVERBEND ART CENTER. Jerry propped their fish poles against the wall to one side of the door and unlatched it. He and Jenny walked into a long, empty room, well lighted by fluorescent lights in the ceiling and by several high windows at the far end. This was the gallery or exhibition hall. The walls were pale gray but they glowed with the color of the many paintings that were displayed on them. Some were dazzling flower arrangements, others were landscapes. There were still lifes of bottles with sunlight pouring through colored glass. There

KARL HOFFMAN

were studies of heads and figures and some paintings that didn't explain themselves. Mother called these "non-representational" art—triangles and squares and oblongs of color arranged in intricate patterns, sometimes pleasing to the eye, sometimes not.

A door opened on the right and Mr. Hoffman called, "Come in. Come in. Let me welcome you to my studio. First we must walk across this classroom and weave our way among the easels of my students. But wait! Even before that we must introduce each other. Me? I am Karl Hoffman, artist, teacher, and renovator of paintings." He bowed. "You, whom I so lately rescued from the appetite of the river, what names are you called by?"

Jerry stepped forward and shook hands. "I am Jeremy Lane," he said. "This is my sister, Jennifer. You know our mother. At least she knows you, for she comes here to paint on Wednesday mornings."

"Oho! Now I have it! The children of Frau Lane, the little lady who paints with such intensity and never wants the morning to end! Yes, she is one of my star pupils. I am most happy to make the acquaintance of her children. Are there more of you at home?"

"We have a little sister. She'll be three in September," said Jenny as they walked across the large studio and entered a smaller room built out over the millrace. "Mother and Dad will sure be grateful to you for rescuing us."

"That was nothing, nothing. I would not like your boat to be broken into matchsticks or for you to be tumbled about in the waterfall and maybe be drowned. At least you might have had your bones snapped in two! No, that would not have been good. I am glad I was on hand at the right moment."

KARL HOFFMAN

"Would it be okay with you not to say anything to our mother about this?" Jerry asked. "You know how mothers are. She might decide it wasn't safe for us to go out in the boat again."

"Not a word! I promise." He smiled at them and his teeth flashed white.

He was a man of medium height, about thirty, rather stockily built. His blond hair was brushed back from a high forehead and grew long on his neck. He wore a navy-and-red-striped jersey tucked into a pair of shabby, paint-smeared jeans. He would be more handsome if he had a haircut, Jenny decided. Even this way he was handsome.

He asked them to open their creel and let him see their fish. While he was admiring their catch, Jenny went to the window from which he had thrown the rope. She looked down on the river flowing silent and deep until it poured in a smooth curve over the lip of the dam. She shivered at what might have happened to them. Jerry was right. It would be better if Mother didn't know. She hoped no one in a car crossing the bridge had recognized them. She shivered again, then turned to look at the painting on the easel near the window.

"You like my picture?" Mr. Hoffman asked.

Jenny nodded. "It's that view from the window, isn't it? The other mill reflected in the river and the steeple of the Methodist Church behind the trees. I like it a lot. My, you use a lot of paint!"

"That is because I painted with a knife. See?" He showed them a little slender trowel-shaped knife at the end of a wooden handle and indicated his palette thick with wiggles of paint. A jar bristling with brushes stood on a small work table near by. There was a pervading smell of turpentine and varnish in the room.

"But you don't always paint with a knife," said Jerry. "You've got a mess of brushes over there in a jar. I never saw so many."

"I paint the way the subject makes me feel. Sometimes smooth and shiny with strokes so fine they hardly show. Sometimes big and bold and splashy with broad sweeps of the brush. Sometimes with thick dabs of paint from the palette knife—like so." He indicated the canvas on the easel.

There were other paintings in their wooden stretchers leaning against the wall, some wrong side to, and there were wooden shelves holding art supplies. In the corner of the room a staircase led up to the artist's living quarters.

"That other thing you are—what does it mean?" asked Jenny.

"Renovator of paintings? Oh, that means to restore or bring back to the original state. Old paintings need

KARL HOFFMAN

to be cleaned. Sometimes age has damaged them. In my own country I worked under one of the great experts in the museum in the city of my birth." His face saddened. "Ach, that is all in the past now. Part of my country is no longer free." He sighed. "Here in this great land of yours, the museums are well staffed with experts. There were no jobs for me. So instead of using my skill in restoring paintings of the past, I create new ones of my own. And that is good, too," he said with a smile. "Especially when my pictures please the eye and people come to buy."

"Are you all alone?" asked Jenny. "Don't you have any family?"

"I had to leave my family behind in East Germany —my father, who teaches in the university, and my mother, and my sister, who is married and has children of her own. Whether I shall ever see them again, I do not know."

"That's tough," said Jerry.

"It was escape or prison for me. I incurred the displeasure of our masters." His voice became bitter. "When my chance came, I took it. I do not like to talk about those times. It makes my heart heavy, here." He touched his chest.

"Maybe they will be able to get away, too, some day," said Jenny hopefully.

"I pray for that time to come," said Karl Hoffman.

"But the way out is difficult and dangerous. I dare not write to them. If they have letters from America, they might be punished for my escape. They do not know where to write to me and I? I do not even know whether they still live. Many of my countrymen have died or disappeared."

The bright-blue eyes were shadowed and there was pain in his voice. He shook himself, as if to push away sad thoughts. "Forgive me! I do not often talk of these things. But you made me think of my nephew and niece at home."

The children were silent, not knowing what to say.

Jenny opened the creel. "I'd like to give you my biggest sunfish for your supper," she said. She could not think of any other way to show her sympathy.

"Thank you, thank you," said Mr. Hoffman, making a formal little bow. "I shall cook it at once, for my lunch! And now you must be off homeward before these fish lose their freshness and before your good mama begins to wonder what keeps you so long. Never fear. She will never learn from me how near you came to getting wet."

He accompanied them to the outside door, where they gathered up their poles and headed home.

After walking some distance in silence, Jenny said, "Maybe we can get Mommy to ask him to dinner. He must get tired of his own cooking."

"I was thinking that, too," said Jeremy.

Debby was waiting for them on the little balcony outside the French windows of the parlor, swinging her legs through the openings in the railing. Mr. Bear sat on one chubby knee peering out. She scrambled to her feet when she saw them open the gate.

"Guess what?" she said. "Racky-Pooh is gone away."

"What!" Jerry dropped the fish poles to the brick walk with a thud.

Debby rested her chin on the top of the railing and looked at them with serious blue eyes. "He's gone. Mommy say he unhooked the door himself. Debby cried."

Jenny noticed tear smudges still on her cheeks. "Mr. Bear won't go away," she comforted. "But raccoons like to be free. Probably Racky-Pooh had a family who needed him. He had to go home to catch fish for his babies."

Debby hugged Mr. Bear close to her. "Mr. Bear Debby's friend," she said. "He stay."

VII

"Tidings of Joy"

Several nights later Mr. Lane came home from his office with an odd sort of smile and a hint of excitement in his manner.

"What has happened?" asked Mrs. Lane, rising from the rocking chair on the porch to greet him at the top of the steps. "You look as though you were bursting with tidings."

"Tidings of joy, I hope," said Mr. Lane, with a smile. "Where are the children? I want them to hear this, too. But let's go into the house."

Jenny and Jerry had been having a game of checkers on the back terrace. They came on the run when Mr.

"TIDINGS OF JOY"

Lane sounded his special whistle. Debby emerged from the parlor where she had been playing with Mr. Bear on the cool floor under the piano.

"Is it about the lost fortune?" asked Jenny.

"Yes," her father said. "I heard from Tracers Company of America today." He produced the letter from his breast pocket. "Come into the living room and let me read it to you. It is postmarked yesterday. 'Dear Mr. Lane,'" he began.

" 'We have your inquiry pertaining to the unclaimed assets of Robert Bancroft Calvert, who died intestate (*That means without making a will*, Mr. Lane explained to the children) at Princeton, New Jersey, in 1930. Mr. Calvert had at one time invested money in the stock of a mining and smelting company. The company went into receivership after the stock market crash of 1929 and later its holdings were absorbed by another company. During the long years of the Depression that followed the crash, no dividends were paid. Now, however, the shares that Robert Bancroft Calvert died believing worthless have regained and increased their value. Today they will bring approximately $27,000, at the present market price.

"We are forwarding your letter to our client, The Delaware Bank and Trust Company of ____ Walnut Street, Philadelphia, custodian of the estate. It will be the bank's task to verify your relationship to the deceased before the claim can be paid. With our good wishes for a happy outcome, we are,

      Very truly yours,
      Tracers Company of America' "

There was a hushed silence when he had finished reading. Mrs. Lane broke the spell. "Twenty-seven thousand dollars!" she exclaimed with awe in her voice.

"Boy, oh boy, oh boy!" shouted Jeremy.

Jenny took hold of Debby and whirled her off her feet around and around until they were both breathless. She let the squealing Debby go and stood before her father panting. "What will we do with it? What will we do with all that money?"

Mr. Lane sobered. He dropped into his favorite wing chair and pulled Debby onto his knee. "Let's not spend it before we have it," he suggested. "I am afraid I have been guilty of the very thing I warned you against: counting chickens! We must not forget that there's the little matter of proof." He gave his head a rueful shake, as if to clear it of impossible dreams. "But to answer your question, Jenny. If, and I underline that 'if,' we should come into all that money, it would go straight into the savings bank where it would earn interest and increase year by year until you children are ready for college. Oh, glory

"TIDINGS OF JOY"

day! You can't begin to realize what it would mean to your mother and me to know that the money for your college education is safe in the bank until we need to use it!"

Jenny made a little face. College seemed far in the future to her. She still had seven more years of grade and high school first. She wished they could spend at least part of the money on something they all wanted and could enjoy right now. A speed boat, for instance, or a sports car. Something glamorous like that. Still it would be a very comfortable feeling to have that amount of money in the bank where it would add to itself through that mysterious process called compound interest. Jenny did not understand how compound interest worked, but she knew it was considered very desirable. She was also aware that at certain times each month when her father was paying the bills, he seemed a bit grim and worried. She had overheard enough adult conversations to realize that financing a college education these days was a real problem. So she said a silent and sensible farewell to visions of speedboats and sports cars and rejoiced with the others.

"What will be the next step?" asked Mrs. Lane.

"Write to the bank, of course. I can't send them the Bible with our family tree, but I can make a copy of that page in it and have it notarized as authentic, or if they want me to, I can photograph it. I'll write tonight." He glanced again at the letter from the Tracers Company. "I wish we knew something more about the Calvert who died in Princeton. We are hanging all our hopes on the single coincidence that the name Bancroft was this Calvert's middle name and my great-great-grandfather's given name. That's really not very much to justify such hopes." His voice lost its confident sound. "We mustn't forget that we can't prove the adoption or the cross switch of names. I really believe the sensible thing would be for us to put the whole thing out of our minds."

Jenny stamped her foot. "Don't you dare, Daddy! Suppose we can't prove it! It won't hurt to write and find out what our chances are. I have a feeling, I really do, that proof will turn up somewhere. What would be the point of Racky-Pooh coming into our house and making such a mess? If he hadn't we would never have seen the notice about the lost fortune. I think we were *meant* to see it!" Jenny's eyes were flashing, her face flushed.

"There's my optimist," said Mr. Lane, smiling up at her. "One other thing. I don't need to remind you and Jerry again that this is a family matter, not to be discussed with anyone else."

Jerry and Jenny nodded. Debby commenced to giggle. "Opti!" she sputtered. "Daddy's opti-MUSS.

"TIDINGS OF JOY"

That a funny, funny thing to be!" She laughed so hard the whole family joined in.

Still laughing, Mrs. Lane got up from the sofa to go to the kitchen. "Supper will be ready in fifteen minutes," she said. "We are going to eat on the terrace. Jenny, will you take Debby up and see that she washes her hands and face? Yours and Jerry's could stand some washing, too," she observed.

As Jenny started upstairs with Debby she heard her father say to Jeremy, "By the way, Son, I hear you and Jenny had quite an adventure on the river Tuesday. Nearly got swept over the dam."

Jenny stopped short, listening, shushing Debby so she could hear.

"How'd you know?" Jerry sounded startled and defensive. "We didn't tell you on purpose 'cause we didn't want you and Mom worried. It turned out all right."

"No fault of yours," Mr. Lane said. "Jake White was going over the bridge and saw you. He dropped by my office today on other business and told me. Said he thought he recognized my kids. Said it was lucky for you Karl Hoffman spotted you and could get a rope over to your boat."

"It sure was lucky for us! Gee, he's a great guy, Dad. We had a wonderful talk with him afterwards. Jen gave him one of her sunfish for his lunch. We wish you and Mom would invite him to dinner sometime. But we didn't know how to go about suggesting it without telling how he rescued us and getting you and Mom all upset."

"That's a good idea. I'll fix it up with Mother. But I'll have to put the river off bounds if you aren't more careful. You'll have to promise me not to let yourself get so close to the dam again."

"Oh, I promise!" said Jerry. "Jen and I have both learned our lesson. We won't ever drift with the current again when we're fishing unless we are way upstream, and we'll keep a close lookout."

"Good," said Dad. "I don't believe a rowboat could actually be swept over the dam except during high water like that we had on Tuesday. But keep away from the dam, just to be on the safe side."

"We will!" said Jerry fervently.

Jenny heaved a sigh of relief. They had gotten off lightly. Dad was more reasonable than Mother in such matters. Since it was all over and they hadn't been hurt and he had made them understand they must be more careful, he hadn't scolded or punished them.

"Come on, Deb. We'll have to hurry now or Jerry will be right on our heels. Don't you tell Mother anything you heard," she added.

VIII

The Quarry

Frannie and Jenny roller-skated with long swooping glides down the worn slate pavement. The even rhythm of their passing was interrupted by the clacking sound as their skates slid over the cracks between the paving stones. They had so much to talk about. Frannie told Jenny all about her visit to the seashore and what fun it had been to swim out beyond the waves and let them carry her into shore. Her nose was peeling, her freckles were swallowed in a warm tan which made her teeth look whiter and her eyes even bluer. Her hair was lighter, too, bleached by sea and sun to the color of corn husks.

"I feel pale beside you," said Jenny enviously. She had been proud of her own tan until now. "Seashore sun does a better job than the sun we have around here, even if it is the same old sun!"

Jenny told Frannie about the exciting day on the river, how they had nearly gone over the dam, and about meeting the artist, Karl Hoffman. "Mother dosen't know about it yet, but Dad's going to get her to ask Mr. Hoffman to dinner some time soon."

Gliding smoothly along the sidewalk by the river wall, they approached the bridge.

"I'm hot," said Frannie. "Let's rest awhile."

They scrambled on top of the wall and sat there, letting the rear wheels of their skates coast up and down the wall as they moved their legs. The entrance to the quarry was directly opposite.

"I know what let's do," said Jenny. She was unfastening her skates as she spoke. "Let's climb the rocks to the top of Quarry Hill."

Frannie undid her skate straps and slid her feet out. Together they crossed the road, dangling their skates by the leather straps.

"We can leave them here," said Jenny, indicating the floor of an old lime kiln cut out of the rock where lime had been burned long ago. They dropped the skates with a clatter and set out, climbing over loose boulders and threading their way through openings between rocks. They had to duck under low-hanging boughs of alders that had grown in crevices where soil had been washed down through the years.

Soon they came to the wall of the quarry which was pitted and uneven, dotted with bushes and streaked with ledges. The going was not difficult at first. The girls were lithe and wiry and they scrambled up over the rocks with ease, their rubber-soled

MYSTERY OF THE HIDDEN FACE

oxfords keeping them from slipping. Gradually the quarry wall grew steeper. Jenny reached for a handhold and pulled herself up onto a narrow ledge where some sparse grass grew. There was just room enough to sit and lean back against the wall behind. Frannie pulled herself up beside Jenny and they gazed out over the way they had come.

"We're almost to the top," said Jenny. "Doesn't Riverbend look small from up here!"

They could look down on the roof of the nearest mill. The crest of the waterfall over the dam was a streak of silver flashing in the sun. The hills far beyond the town were a smoky-blue, the sky soft with lazy clouds. Riverbend seemed a toy village encircled by the glinting water of the river. Rooftops shown in varicolored patches through the green of trees. Cars moving across the bridge below and the highway bridge farther downstream were not much larger than shiny beetles.

Jenny drew a deep breath. "Don't you love to be up high like this?" She tossed a pebble over the ledge and after a minute heard it land below.

Frannie did not answer. She was so silent Jenny turned to see why. Her friend had pressed herself as close to the wall as she could get, her knees drawn up, away from the edge. Her freckles stood out from the suddenly faded color of her face. She looked half sick.

THE QUARRY

"What on earth's the matter?" asked Jenny.

"I'm scared! It makes me dizzy to look down. It's so far! Suppose we should slip? Oh, I wish I hadn't come." These last words were a wail.

"Now, Frannie, don't be scared. Keep your eyes away from the edge. We haven't far to go. You won't fall. Come, let's get up and move along this ledge and try to find which way we go from here. You follow me. I won't let anything happen to you."

Frannie gulped a sob and rubbed her eyes. "I'm sorry, Jen. I'll try not to panic. I just didn't know what it would be like."

Jenny got to her feet, keeping one hand on the rough stone behind her, and started edging her way along the ledge. "Keep your face to the wall," she told Frannie, "and slide your feet along like this toward me. There's a ledge just above this that won't be hard to get to. I see a good hold just a few steps further where a bush is growing out of a crack. You can get a toe hold there and pull yourself up. I'll go first and show you. Just watch and do exactly as I do."

Little by little they made their way to the place where the shrub grew from the rock. Jenny tested it. It was firmly rooted. With the fingers of one hand grasping the ledge above, she placed one foot into a crotch of the sturdy trunk of the shrub and lifted herself, rolling onto the ledge.

"Come on now, Fran. You can do it, too." Jenny stretched out on her stomach, hooking her toes over an outcrop of rock near the base of the wall, and reached down a hand to Frannie.

Frannie compressed her lips, shut her eyes tight for a moment, making a visible effort to overcome her fear. Then, gripping Jenny's hand, she placed one foot in the same crotch of the shrub. Jenny pulled for all she was worth and together they managed to heave Frannie upward onto the ledge. There she lay, gasping and sweating.

"This is a much wider ledge," said Jenny. "You can roll back to the wall and sit up and you won't have to look over the edge. You did fine, Frannie. Just rest a while now while I try to decide what we do next."

"Oh, Jenny, I don't think I could make it again. My heart is pounding so I feel as though I'd choke!"

Jenny looked at her worriedly. She knew some people were unreasonably (at least it seemed unreasonable to her) afraid of heights, but she had never suspected Frannie was one of them. She felt terribly responsible. If Frannie could not make herself go on, what would they do? It would be impossible to backtrack now. Going down the way they had come would be twice as dangerous and much more scary. They were so near the top, too.

Jenny examined their position. This ledge, she saw,

THE QUARRY

was like a rounded doorstep protruding from the wall of the quarry. It slanted upward on her left, but to the right—just a few feet beyond where Frannie lay—it curved inward to the rock face. They couldn't go that way. There was nothing but empty space below.

Above their heads the rock jutted outward. That was the frustrating thing—it meant there was no chance of going straight up even though the distance was so short. There remained only the ledge to the left sloping gently upward until it curved around a shoulder of rock and was lost to view.

"Frannie, I've got to explore a little. Will you just stay here quietly until I come back? Don't move. You'll be all right."

"Oh, Jen! Do you have to go?"

Jenny nodded. "I've got to find out where we go from here. We can't go straight up because of the way the rock bulges out. This ledge bends around that rocky shoulder there. I want to find out how far it goes. I won't be more than a minute."

"If you're any longer than that I'll start to scream."

"Oh no you won't! What good would that do? It might startle me and make me slip! You be getting your second wind while I am gone. I'll be quick. Promise."

In no time at all Jenny was back. She wore such a strange expression Frannie sat up in alarm.

MYSTERY OF THE HIDDEN FACE

"Wha— What's the matter? You look as if you'd seen something."

"I have," said Jenny.

"But what? Doesn't the ledge go on up?"

"That's just what. It doesn't. From here it looks as though it would, but when I came to where it bends around the rock there, I got a nasty shock. It narrows down to nothing. I couldn't go any further. The most maddening thing is that the top is just beyond reach."

Frannie looked at her despairingly. Finally she asked, "What does that mean?"

Jenny lowered herself beside Frannie, stretched her legs out, and shoved her shoulders against the wall. She avoided Frannie's anxious gaze, staring straight ahead into space. Finally she drew a deep breath. "It means," she said, "that we'll just have to sit here and wait until someone misses us and comes to find us."

There was a stunned silence. Before Frannie could break it, Jenny went on. "We're so close to the top it's sickening. But I couldn't find a crack or a toe hold we could use to climb that last stretch. Oh, Frannie, I'm so terribly sorry I got you into this mess. I thought I remembered the way up. Jerry and I have both climbed here before. But I must have taken a wrong turn somewhere down below." She threw one arm around Frannie's shoulders. "We're sure to be missed soon. Both our mothers expected us home for lunch.

THE QUARRY

When we don't come, Jerry or Tom will be sent to look for us. When we see them we can call to them. It must be past lunchtime now, I'm so hungry."

IX

Another Rescue

It happened very much as Jenny had foreseen. First there was a call from Mrs. Jordan to Mrs. Lane asking what was keeping Frannie so long; it was past lunchtime. Mrs. Lane told her that Jennifer had not come home either and said she would send Jeremy to look for them.

Jerry grabbed a handful of cookies as he went through the kitchen. He wheeled his bike down the front walk and out the gate. Before he mounted it he looked up and down the street. There were no skating figures to be seen anywhere. *Chances are they are gabbing together by the bridge before they separate*

ANOTHER RESCUE

to go home, he thought. Frannie and Tom lived on a farm reached by the river road beyond the Riverbend Art Center. The bridge would be a natural place for the girls to part. He didn't see why their stomachs hadn't told them it was long past the hour for lunch.

He came to the Riverbend House without meeting anyone who had seen them. Beyond, the sidewalk to the bridge was empty. He peddled slowly to the entrance to the bridge, trying to decide whether to cross on over into the business section of town or to follow the river road. Perhaps Jenny was seeing Frannie all the way home.

As he hesitated his eye caught a flash of light coming from the floor of one of the old lime kilns in the quarry. That was odd. It must be sunlight striking something shiny like metal, but what sort of thing? He'd better have a look.

Jerry dismounted and pushed his bike into the quarry. There on the lime-kiln floor he found his sister's and Frannie's skates. Even as he bent to look at them, he heard Jenny's voice sounding far away, "Jerry, help! We're up here on a ledge and we can't get down!"

He finally spied them—two huddled figures high on the craggy wall, sitting close together on a shelf of rock. Their predicament was plain to be seen.

Cupping his hands around his mouth he shouted

"Don't move! I'll try to get Mr. Hoffman."

As Jerry ran across the road he noticed a dusty sedan parked outside the mill. The gallery was empty. He hurried across the classroom to the door of Karl Hoffman's studio and burst into the room, interrupting a conversation between the artist and two men. "Mr. Hoffman," he said, "Jenny and Frannie are stuck on a ledge way up on the quarry and can't get down. Will you get your rope and come quick!"

There was an uncomfortable silence in the room. He was aware that the two men had turned their backs and were sliding a large flat package into one of the upright storage bins where canvases and stretchers were kept. Mr. Hoffman had a strange expression on his face. He didn't seem his usual friendly self. "It would be better, another time, to knock, Jeremy," he said, very quietly.

"Gee, I'm sorry, Mr. Hoffman! I didn't mean to butt in when you were busy, but this is an—an emergency."

"I assume that it must be," said Mr. Hoffman. "Gentlemen, will you please to excuse me? I think you have made your meaning clear. I have no choice."

The bulkier of the two men half turned toward them. He spoke in a husky low voice, not looking at Mr. Hoffman or Jeremy. "There should be no room for misunderstanding." The words sounded harmless

ANOTHER RESCUE

enough, yet Jerry had the fleeting impression that they concealed a threat.

He opened the door and waited while Mr. Hoffman lifted the coil of rope from a nail on the wall. It was the same rope he had used to rescue them from the river. They left the room without saying good-by to the visitors. Not until much later did Jerry realize that he had not really seen the faces of either of the men.

Once they were out of the mill, Karl Hoffman drew a deep breath and looked down at Jerry. "Tell me now of this difficulty of your sister's. She is safe on a ledge, you say, but cannot go either up or down?" His voice was again warm and friendly.

"That's it. Let's cross the road and I'll show you." Jerry led him to where he could see for himself the two girls on their shelf of rock. He shouted up to them, "We're coming, Mr. Hoffman and me, just give us time."

"You see how high they are," he said to Mr. Hoffman. "They can't make that last little stretch because the rock overhangs. And they are afraid to climb down."

"I can't say that I blame them," said Mr. Hoffman. "How are we going to get to them? Is there any other way to the top?"

"Yes. Do you see how the quarry ends just beyond

the mill? We can go down the river road a way and climb the hill from there, where it isn't nearly as steep. Come on."

Jerry led the way down the road under the willow trees to a place where they could scramble up the hillside through underbrush. They came out on open fields that swept up to the lip of the quarry. The sun shone full upon them as they hurried up the slope, trampling daisies and buttercups underfoot. They arrived hot and flushed at the spot they thought must be near where the girls were stranded. Jerry called out and Jenny answered, pinpointing their position.

Karl Hoffman's eyes measured the distance from the edge of the quarry to the nearest tree, a stunted oak that grew some yards back. The rope would easily reach that far.

They threw themselves on the ground and pushed forward until they could look over the edge. The girls were not visible. All they could see were Jenny's dirty scuffed saddle oxfords and socks and a stretch of sunburned legs. The rock hid the ledge and the rest of her.

"We are just above you, Jennifer," said Karl Hoffman. "I can see only part of you. Are you both all right?"

"I guess so," said Jenny. "At least I think I am." Her voice did not sound too sure. "Frannie's dizzy.

ANOTHER RESCUE

She doesn't like being up so high. And it's so far down we can't help being sort of scared. We thought you'd never get here!"

"We came as fast as we could," said Mr. Hoffman. "Tell me now, how near are you to the top? Does the ledge go any farther in either direction? Describe it to me."

Jenny's legs and feet disappeared. "Here where we are it's about three feet, I'd say, above my head to where the rock juts out." Her voice sounded stronger and closer and they realized she must be standing. "The ledge is wide enough where we are and it slopes upward to the left. Then it gets narrower until it comes to a shoulder of rock. Do you see where I mean?"

Jerry and Karl Hoffman quickly spotted the place. The rock formed a smooth vertical column down to the ledge. Best of all, there was no overhang. This would be the place for the rescue.

"We can get you up easily from there," said Mr. Hoffman.

"The trouble is, Frannie's petrified to move."

"Frannie, listen to me," said Mr. Hoffman. "You'll be up here with us in no time if you do exactly as I say. I'm going to lower my rope with a loop tied in the end. Jenny will help you slip it over your head and under your arms. Then you must stand up and face the wall. Keep your eyes fixed on it. We'll keep tight hold of our end of the rope and follow along with you. We won't let you fall. Do you understand?"

Frannie's voice came to them faintly. "I'll try. I'll do just as you say." Jerry could tell she was making an effort to be brave.

ANOTHER RESCUE

The rope slithered over the edge. Jenny caught hold of it and helped Frannie put her head and arms through it. "This does make me feel safer," Frannie told her. "You go first."

"No," said Jennie. "You must be the first one up. Slowly stand, now, and move toward me. I'll step around you. Face the wall the way Mr. Hoffman said and sidestep slowly. Keep your hands touching the rock. I'll be right beside you."

The rope tautened as Frannie moved. She felt its support as she began her slow sideways progress. When they came to the rock shoulder, Frannie could almost reach the top with her fingertips. Karl Hoffman's head appeared. "You are going to have to help yourself some more, Frannie. Do you have rubber soles on your shoes? Good. When we start to pull, you must push your toes against the rock, first one and then the other, as if you were walking up the wall. Wait one further moment now while we secure our end of the rope around a tree trunk here, so it can't get away from us." Frannie's heart beat hard and she closed her eyes while she waited. In no time Karl Hoffman asked, "Are you ready?"

"As ready as I ever shall be!"

"All right then."

She felt the tug of the rope as they pulled from above. She toed her shoes against the wall, one step—

MYSTERY OF THE HIDDEN FACE

then another, reaching with her fingers for the top. She touched grass. In another minute her head rose above the quarry edge and she could see Mr. Hoffman kneeling a little distance from the edge, Jerry just behind him. The muscles stood out on Mr. Hoffman's forearms as he kept the rope taut.

Frannie dug her elbows into the earth. Then it was safe for Jerry to let go his hold on the rope and reach for her hands. Together he and Mr. Hoffman pulled her to safety. She lay prone on the good, firm earth and took a long shuddering breath before gasping out her thanks.

They gave her a moment to recover. Then the rope was lowered to Jenny and in a few more anxious moments she, too, was safe.

Mrs. Lane was surprised to see from the kitchen window Jennifer and Frannie straggling down the sloping back yard from Quarry Hill, their knees and elbows scraped and bleeding.

"Where have you been? Did Jerry find you? How did you hurt yourselves?"

They told her. She listened with dismay. "You go up to the bathroom and I'll be right along to clean your scratches and put some antiseptic on them. But first I must telephone Mrs. Jordan so she'll know Frannie's here. You say Jerry is bringing your skates when he comes?"

ANOTHER RESCUE

Jenny nodded. Mother had not scolded yet. She was too glad to have them home safe, but Jennie knew her mother would have something to say.

While they ate sandwiches and soup, Mrs. Lane sat with them, not speaking. The two girls were too hungry to waste time in talk.

"My, that was good!" said Frannie. She looked at Mrs. Lane's unsmiling face. "Please don't be mad at Jenny."

"I'm not mad," said Mrs. Lane. "Just thankful you are both whole and in one piece. Jenny, you should have known better! You may have some Rocky Mountain goat in you, but you had no business taking Frannie on any such adventure. Suppose you had lost your footing? Suppose Jerry hadn't found you, or Mr. Hoffman hadn't been there with a rope?"

"Don't go on supposing!" said Jenny. "Jerry *did* find us. Mr. Hoffman *was* there, and here we are only a few scratches the worse. I'm sorry I took Frannie. I didn't know she was scared of high places. And I won't ever do it again."

"All right," said Mrs. Lane. "I'm going to drive Frannie home now. I'll try to explain to her mother that you didn't intend to do anything dangerous. But you, my girl, are going to be grounded for a while. You may go to your room now and stay there until you hear Debby wake up from her nap. And you are not to leave the house or yard."

Jennie went upstairs and flopped on her bed. She supposed Mother had a right to be annoyed. As she thought back over their experience she could appreciate that they had had a narrow squeak. If either of them had lost her balance, a fall to that rocky quarry floor could have been the end. She knew she had a bad habit of rushing into things without thinking of the consequences. Daddy said she was "impetuous"—that she never recognized danger. She remembered the time Mother had found her sitting with a book on a narrow unfenced roof over a bay window in their old house. She supposed it had looked precarious from Mother's place on the sidewalk, but Jenny herself had felt perfectly safe and not the least afraid of falling off. There had been times, too, when she had climbed awfully high in trees. Once a branch had torn loose and she had fallen, but luckily she landed on the branch and escaped with no bones broken.

She heard the screen door slam and Jerry whistling below. Presently he came to the foot of the stairs and called, "Jen, where are you?"

"In my room. Mother said I had to stay here till Debby wakes up."

He came bounding up the stairs and lounged in the doorway.

"That was a fool stunt you pulled."

ANOTHER RESCUE

"Don't rub it in. I know it. Mr. Hoffman has saved our necks twice now. Say, do I hear Debby? Let's put her in her bathing suit and give her a swim in the plastic tub in the yard."

X

A Letter from Philadelphia

Being grounded was not too hard on Jenny. Of course it meant no swimming, but since it rained on Tuesday no one else went swimming anyway. Instead, she ironed all the dish towels, handkerchiefs, and napkins for her mother, which made her feel very useful. It was pleasant in the kitchen with the rain scurrying down the window panes and drumming a tattoo on the terrace awning.

Mrs. Lane let Jenny make popovers for lunch. She whizzed the ingredients in the blender—eggs, milk, flour, salt, and melted butter—then poured the liquid into the deep cups of the iron popover pan. It was

A LETTER FROM PHILADELPHIA

fun watching through the oven window as the contents of each cup lifted gradually, rising higher and higher and becoming all brown and crusty on top. She held Debby up for her to see, too.

When Mr. Lane came home for lunch he was delighted to have this unexpected treat. But Debby was disappointed because the popovers were hollow inside. However, when she tasted their buttery goodness smeared with strawberry jam, she wanted another right away.

Jenny had the pleased sense that she was making up to her mother for the worry she had caused her. She promised herself silently not to get into any more trouble.

After lunch, while Debby had her nap, Jenny talked with Frannie on the phone. Frannie's mother had gotten over her scare about their dangerous experience, but she had made Frannie promise never to go into the quarry again. Frannie chuckled when she told Jenny this. "As if I'd ever want to!" she said.

On Wednesday while Mrs. Lane was at her painting class, Jenny took Debby to Grandmother Turner's on Leigh Street to the house where their mother had lived when she was a little girl. It was a wide, comfortable house with two bay windows on either side of the front porch and a stairway with a wonderful bannister to slide down. Best of all, it had a deep back yard with a barn, and behind the barn a garden, and beyond the garden Beaver Brook where Jenny and Debby could wade and paddle and build dams.

Grandmother Turner was a brisk, lively lady who seemed younger than her years. Her leaf-brown hair had no touch of gray. She had a quick laugh and she was always busy, gardening, playing bridge, going to meetings, or entertaining. But Wednesday was her day to stay at home, to bake bread, and to keep an eye on her youngest grandchild while Debby's mother painted.

Jenny and Jerry could take care of themselves, but no matter what activity they might be involved in with their friends, they always turned up at Grandmother Turner's when the loaves of bread were due to come out of the oven. The smell was heavenly! Grandmother cut them warm slices which they buttered and sprinkled with granulated sugar. Nothing ever tasted so good. Sometimes Grandmother hid presents in the dough—a little charm for Jenny's bracelet, or a shiny new dime, or a tiny whistle—and sent the loaf with surprises home with the children.

Today, when Jenny and Debby arrived at Grandmother's, they found their mother's younger sister Ruth. She greeted Jenny and Debby with hugs and kisses and told them she had come to spend part of

A LETTER FROM PHILADELPHIA

her vacation before setting off on an automobile trip with friends.

Aunt Ruth was one of the Lane children's favorite people. She was fair of hair and complexion like their mother, with a merry tilt to her lips and a gay bubbling laugh—in spite of tragedy that had touched her personal life. The man to whom she had been engaged had not returned from border duty in Korea. He had been killed by a sniper's bullet. Though she had had other suitors, Aunt Ruth had not married. Jenny and Jeremy wished that she would. She was seven years younger than Mrs. Lane, and they thought that thirty was a ripe old age for matrimony and that she'd better hurry or she'd be a real old maid. She had that wonderful art of being interested in everything and of making other people feel at ease. When you talked, she listened as though she thought whatever you said was really important. This was a quality that was especially appreciated by Jenny, for she had not encountered it too frequently in grown-ups.

Aunt Ruth put on her bathing suit and joined Jenny and Debby at the brook, where she sun-bathed on a beach towel as they splashed and paddled. While Debby played with pebbles and sticks at the brook's edge Jenny sat cross-legged near Aunt Ruth and told her about being grounded because of the quarry adventure. She also told how Karl Hoffman had rescued

MYSTERY OF THE HIDDEN FACE

her and Jeremy from going over the dam, and about his family behind the Iron Curtain and how sad he was not to know what had happened to them.

"He sounds like a real friend in need," said Aunt Ruth, "and perhaps in need of a friend himself."

"He's real keen to look at, too," said Jenny. "I mean he'd be handsome if he had a haircut."

Aunt Ruth laughed. "Maybe you can persuade him to," she said.

Mrs. Lane came for Jenny and Debby at lunchtime and invited Aunt Ruth for dinner the following night. "I've asked Karl Hoffman, my art teacher. I want you to meet him."

"Jenny's been singing his praises," said Aunt Ruth.

"He's rather shy," said Mrs. Lane. "That's because he's lived by himself so long, I expect. He doesn't go out much. He didn't want me to thank him for coming to your rescue, Jenny. I have a notion he wouldn't accept this invitation if it weren't for you and Jeremy. He likes you!"

"That shows he has good taste," said Aunt Ruth.

Jenny beamed. "He'll like you, too," she said. "Oh, I'm so glad you asked him, Mommy, and he said he would come!"

That evening after Debby had been put to bed, Mr. Lane told the rest of the family that he had received a letter from the bank in Philadelphia. It con-

A LETTER FROM PHILADELPHIA

tained disappointing news. "Just as I feared," he said. "There is another Calvert relative who believes he is the missing heir and is entitled to Robert Bancroft Calvert's money."

"Oh, no!" said Mrs. Lane. "Who is he?"

"His name is Joseph Hart Calvert. The bank says he has furnished satisfactory legal evidence of his relationship."

Jenny was stunned. Even though Daddy had warned that there might be someone else who had a better claim than theirs, she had not really believed there would be.

"What else did the letter say?" Mrs. Lane asked.

"It's rather too long and complicated to read to the children, but I learned a lot from it." He handed the letter to his wife. "It told me that Robert Bancroft Calvert, who died in Princeton in 1930, was a bachelor. He was born in 1850, the son of Brevard Calvert who was a younger brother of my great-great-grandfather, Bancroft Calvert. Oh, if I could only prove that relationship! But this Joseph Calvert is able to prove that he is descended from a first cousin of Bancroft and Brevard Calvert, a child of their father's brother. That would make him a very distant cousin of mine. Queer to think of, isn't it? Neither of us knew the other existed before we made our claims."

With the letter open in her hand Mrs. Lane had

MYSTERY OF THE HIDDEN FACE

been listening intently to her husband. "But Henry," she said, "if Joseph is descended from a first cousin of Brevard Calvert, that is not as close a relationship as yours. You are descended from Brevard's brother!"

"Let me have the letter again," said Mr. Lane. "I'll read what the bank has to say about that. Here it is—the next to last paragraph." He held the letter nearer the light and read.

> "While your own relationship to the deceased appears to be closer, since you trace your descent from a brother of Brevard Calvert, father of the deceased, instead of from a first cousin, we must have incontrovertible legal proof that your great-grandfather Henry Calvert Lane was the child of Melissa Lane and Bancroft Calvert and that his name was subsequently changed from Calvert to Lane when he was adopted, or went to live with his uncle, Charles Lane. Without such proof we have no choice but to award the estate of the late Robert Bancroft Calvert to the claimant, Joseph Hart Calvert."

Mrs. Lane made a sound like a groan. "Then it doesn't look as though we had a chance, does it?" she said.

"That's how I size it up," said Mr. Lane.

Jerry looked at Jenny. Her mouth was drooping, her eyes big with dismay. He hesitated, then asked the question that was weighing on his mind. "Does that

A LETTER FROM PHILADELPHIA

mean we won't be able to go to college?"

Mr. Lane gave back the letter to his wife, then turned a serious face to Jerry. "No, it doesn't mean that, Son. It does mean that college won't be quite as easy to manage. We'll have to be economical, resist spending money on things we don't really need, save all we can. You'll have to help, too. When you are old enough, you'll have to find a summer job. But"—he smiled at both children—"work never hurt anyone yet. We are back just where we were before we ever heard about this money and your mother and I had every intention of helping you get a college education then. You and Jennifer must study hard and get the best marks in school you can. Perhaps you'll qualify for scholarships. That would help enormously. Now the thing for us to do is to put this lost fortune out of our minds and forget about it, because as far as I can see there is no possible way to prove we are entitled to it."

Mrs. Lane had finished reading the letter. She looked up at her husband. "At least the bank isn't going to do anything final right away," she said. "They are going to give us some more time to find proof, if we can."

"A lot of good that will do us," said Mr. Lane. "I've even been over the town records of births and deaths at the county clerk's office. There was nothing to help us there. And there's no other place to look for proof that I can think of."

That was the end of the conversation. Jenny went dejectedly into the kitchen to drink a glass of milk before she went to bed. On the way back she switched on the dining room light and stood for a long time before the portrait of Phoebe King Lane. The penetrating blue eyes behind the steel-rimmed glasses returned her gaze but told her nothing. The thin lips were pressed together as though they were closed upon a secret.

"Oh," thought Jenny despairingly, "if only I could make you talk."

XI

Something "Funny-Peculiar"

Karl Hoffman arrived promptly at six o'clock on Thursday evening. For the first time Jenny and Jerry saw him in clothes other than faded dungarees. He wore a light blue pin-striped seersucker suit with a white shirt and plain blue tie. His hair was brushed smooth, and had been trimmed; his eyes seemed more vividly blue in his fresh-scrubbed face.

"Gee, you look NEAT!" said Jerry, shaking hands at the top of the porch steps.

"I hardly know myself," said Mr. Hoffman, smiling. "It is not often I go out to dinner."

Jennifer had been commanded by Mother not to

wear shorts so she put on her pink chambray with full skirt and puffed sleeves. She had washed her hair, brushed it till it shone, and tied it in a high pony tail with a pink ribbon. Mr. Hoffman gazed at her as if he couldn't believe his eyes.

"Can this be Jenny? Or is it a rose strayed in from the garden?"

SOMETHING "FUNNY-PECULIAR"

Jenny's cheeks grew pink. Then she giggled. A rose with patches on its knees and elbows! But she couldn't help being pleased. No one had ever compared her to a rose before.

"Ha, ha," snorted Jerry. "A rose with thorns!"

"Come in, come in," said Mrs. Lane from the front doorway. "We are so happy to see you."

They followed her into the living room where Mr. Lane and Aunt Ruth were waiting. "You know Henry. This is my sister, Ruth Turner. She teaches school in Maine and does not get home half often enough."

There was more handshaking. Jenny thought Aunt Ruth looked especially pretty tonight in a pale green sleeveless linen dress.

"I've heard so many nice things about you I am delighted to meet you," she said. "My sister says your class is wonderful. And you have two firm admirers here." She rested a hand on Jerry's and Jenny's shoulders.

"It is—how do you say—mutual?" said Mr. Hoffman, laughing. "But is there not another member of this family? I remember hearing of a little sister."

"Oh, Debby!" said Jenny. "She's out in the kitchen, but she must be finished her supper now. I'll go get her."

Mother excused herself, too, and followed Jenny

to start putting the dinner on. Jenny wiped Debby's mouth with her bib, lifted the tray of her high chair, and helped her down. "Good girl. You didn't get your dress dirty. Come on, you're going to meet Mr. Hoffman now."

"Tell Jerry he may light the candles," said her mother. "We're going to eat indoors because it looks so showery."

Dinner was a festive meal. Candlelight shone on Mrs. Lane's best linen and silver and china. Mr. Lane carved generous portions of roast chicken and spooned savory stuffing on each plate before it was passed to Mrs. Lane to receive a serving of mashed potatoes and peas. Aunt Ruth ladled the gravy and Jenny passed the hot rolls and jelly.

"Nothing, positively nothing, ever tasted so good!" said Mr. Hoffman after his first forkful.

"Jenny was sure roast chicken would be something you wouldn't cook for yourself," said Mrs. Lane.

"She couldn't be more correct. My cooking runs to hamburgs and frankfurters and those easy frozen dinners you buy at the store."

Jenny and Jerry listened to the grown-up talk and laughter while they polished off their plates. Debby was being very good. They could glimpse her in the living room in her small rocking chair pretending to read a book to Mr. Bear. Mother had promised to let

SOMETHING "FUNNY-PECULIAR"

her have ice cream and cake with them, but only on condition she keep quiet and amuse herself while her elders ate.

As Mr. Lane carved second helpings Mr. Hoffman said, "The old lady on the wall—I have been admiring her. Is she a member of this family?"

"She's the ancestor Jenny and Jerry found in the attic the day we moved into the house," said Mrs. Lane.

"She's our four-times-great-grandma," said Jenny. "Do you mind her looking at you?"

Karl Hoffman laughed. "No, but she does have a fierce gaze!"

"I used to think she could tell when I'd been bad," said Jerry. "I still don't like to face her at the table."

"We don't know who painted her," said Mr. Lane. "Her name was Phoebe King. She married my great-great-great-grandfather Lane and lived to be ninety-four. I don't know what year this was painted, but she must have been pretty old at the time."

Mr. Hoffman studied the portrait. "I don't think so," he said. "Note how firm is the flesh beneath her chin. It does not sag as in the throat of an old lady. Her hands are plump. Not well painted like her face, but that is probably because the artist did not know how to paint hands well. I would say she was a woman in her late middle years or a little older."

"I believe you are right," said Mrs. Lane. "Women dressed like old ladies at a much earlier age then than we do now. I wish after dinner you would take a good look at the portrait. There's a crack in the board on which it is painted. I wonder if it could be repaired."

"Mr. Hoffman is the man to fix it, if it can be," piped Jenny. "He used to restore paintings in a museum in his own country."

"It is quite a fine example of American primitive painting," said Mr. Hoffman. "I'll be glad to have a closer look at it after dinner, and to try to restore it if you wish."

Mrs. Lane was embarrassed. "Some day we might be able to afford to have it restored," she said, "but not right now."

Aunt Ruth changed the subject. "Speaking of paintings," she said, "do you have any theory about all of the art thefts that have been taking place from museums and private collections both in this country and in Europe? I cannot for the life of me see how any thief of a famous painting could hope to sell it. It would surely be recognized."

Mr. Hoffman shook his head. "A terrible thing. Terrible." He seemed oddly agitated.

"Remember that Goya portrait taken from the National Gallery in London some time ago? No trace

SOMETHING "FUNNY-PECULIAR"

of it has ever been found," said Aunt Ruth.

"No trace," said Mr. Lane. "But there were several letters offering to return it on payment of some enormous sum of money. That suggests it is being held for ransom."

"Crank letters, I suspect," said Mrs. Lane. "No ransom has been paid and the painting is still missing."

"I read somewhere that a number of stolen Picassos, Renoirs, and Cezannes and other French paintings worth a fabulous amount had been discovered by detectives from Scotland Yard. The paintings were in a warehouse hidden under a blanket," said Aunt Ruth.

"I can't see how an art theft like that could bring its perpetrators any profit," said Mr. Lane. *Why did Daddy use such big words?* Jenny wondered. "It would be impossible to dispose of them."

"I wonder. There was another case in the papers just recently. Paintings taken from a mansion in St. Louis. Could some private collector in another country buy them, no questions asked, if they could be smuggled out of the U.S.A.?" Aunt Ruth looked to Mr. Hoffman for an answer.

"I wish I knew! It is all very puzzling." He took a handkerchief from his pocket and patted his forehead, Jenny noticed. It wasn't that warm in here. This talk of stolen paintings was exciting. She was disappointed to have her mother signal her to remove the plates. Aunt Ruth started to rise from her chair.

"No, Ruth, Jenny and I can manage. Stay where you are," Mrs. Lane said.

"Ice cream now?" asked a small voice from the living room.

"Come on in, Deb," said Mr. Lane. "You've been a very good girl. You may join us now."

Debby appeared in the doorway, her eyes sparkling. She went straight to Karl Hoffman. "I like you," she said.

"And I like you!" He drew her up onto his knee.

"Deb's a charmer," laughed Aunt Ruth.

Soon they were all enjoying strawberry ice cream and angel cake and the talk switched from stolen paintings to other things.

Before the grown-ups went to the living room to have coffee, the sidelights were turned on and Mr. Hoffman examined the portrait. "The paint has flaked off here and there," he said, "and the crack extends almost the length of the board. That will not be difficult to correct. Some glue with clamps to hold the edges rigidly together while the glue dries, a bit of filling in and retouching where the paint is gone—a simple matter. Just let me know when you would like to have it done."

"Sometime we'll call on you," said Mrs. Lane. "It

SOMETHING "FUNNY-PECULIAR"

is good to know that there is an expert right here in town when we are ready."

Jenny and Jerry were allowed to stay up later than usual. When they went reluctantly to bed Mr. Hoffman and Aunt Ruth were still there.

Jenny lay in her bed wide-eyed in the dark, reliving the evening, remembering the dinner-table talk, and feeling oddly troubled. Presently there came a muffled tap on her door and a whispered, "Are you awake?"

"Yes, come in." She switched on the bedside light.

Jerry opened the door, closed it silently, and plopped himself on the foot of the bed. Jenny drew up her knees, leaned on one elbow, head on hand, watching him.

"Did something strike you as funny-peculiar tonight at the table?" Jerry asked.

"How do you mean?"

"Did you notice Mr. Hoffman when Aunt Ruth began to talk about all those art thefts?"

Jenny sat up and leaned forward, hugging her pajama-clad knees. She nodded slowly. "Yes, I did. He seemed sort of—I don't know how to put it—ill at ease, maybe. It wasn't hot in the room. At least I didn't think so. But he took out his handkerchief and mopped his forehead."

"I noticed that, too," said Jerry. "It made me wonder. And then I remembered something that happened the day you climbed the quarry."

"What? Why didn't you tell me?"

"I guess I forgot it because of all the excitement and bother of getting you and Frannie off that ledge."

"Well, tell me now. What happened?" Jenny's eyes were worried.

"It was another sort of funny-peculiar thing," said Jerry. "There were two men in his studio when I busted in without knocking. They'd been talking, but as soon as I opened the door they stopped, as if they didn't want me to hear. The two men whirled around so all I saw was their backs. Mr. Hoffman looked at me in a queer way—cold, I guess you'd call it. And he said something about it would be better another time to knock. Gee, I was embarrassed, but I had to get him to come. He didn't introduce me to his friends. They seemed to be all-fired busy shoving something into one of those upright storage compartments. There was hardly any conversation. He just said something about their meaning being clear and that he had 'no choice.' The whole thing was uncomfortable. One of the men said there should be 'no room for misunderstanding.' I could hardly wait to get outside, and when we did, Mr. Hoffman was just like his old self again."

Jenny was silent, her face troubled.

SOMETHING "FUNNY-PECULIAR"

"Do you think what I am thinking?" Jerry asked finally.

"I don't *want* to think what you're thinking." Jenny was vehement. "I can't bear to believe that he'd do anything bad like that unless, like he said, he has no choice. But doesn't everyone have a choice? Between right and wrong, I mean? What do you suppose he meant?"

"I don't know. But when you get to thinking about it, it all sort of fits together. Those men hiding something when I butted into the room. And sort of threatening him. And his being a restorer of paintings. And then, the way he acted tonight."

Jenny half sighed, half groaned. "There must be some other explanation," she said. "People come all the time to see the art exhibits or to buy paintings. What did the two men look like? Would you recognize them if you saw them again?"

"One was shorter and bigger around than the other. That's all I know. They took good care that I wouldn't get a good look at them."

"Gosh, this is awful," said Jenny. "First we find out there's no hope of Dad's proving he's the missing heir, and now this. What can we do?"

Jeremy shrugged. "I don't suppose there's anything we can do," he said. "Except keep our eyes open and hope that we're completely wrong. We could be, you know." He stood up, stretched, and yawned widely. "Me for the sack. At least I feel better having talked it over with you. Good night, Sis."

XII

"Against My Will"

Jerry and Jenny kept their suspicions to themselves. They learned from their mother that Karl Hoffman had walked Aunt Ruth home that night and that the two had seemed to hit it off very well together. Jenny ordinarily would have been having all sorts of pleasant fantasies about a possible romance between Aunt Ruth and Karl Hoffman, but with the inner worry gnawing at her mind, she wasn't sure she wanted Aunt Ruth to like him that much. From what Mother told her they seemed to be seeing a good deal of one another.

Several weeks passed with the usual summer activities—tennis, swimming, fishing, cookouts and picnic parties. Jenny and Frannie spent the night at each other's houses. Jerry and Tom went on expeditions together. In spite of these good times, underneath the surface Jenny and Jerry were always uneasy. As often as possible they walked by the Riverbend Art Center, their eyes alert for a dusty sedan with two strange men.

On Friday as they passed the mill on the way to their boat Mr. Hoffman hailed them in an excited voice from his studio window. "Jenny, Jeremy, come in! You must hear my news. The most wonderful thing has happened!"

They tore through the gallery and across the classroom to his private quarters. He stood there, holding a yellow sheet of paper, his face dazed.

"You will never believe! I cannot believe it myself. Read this! It just came. My family, they are safe!"

The sheet of paper was a cablegram from the International Red Cross. It announced that Karl Hoffman's parents, his sister, her husband and children, had reached safety in West Berlin.

Jenny jumped up and down with joy. "How wonderful! Oh, I'm so glad!"

"That's great! Simply great!" said Jerry. He pumped Mr. Hoffman's hand up and down and then the artist grabbed both children and waltzed them

"AGAINST MY WILL"

round and round the studio.

"It is too good to be true! It is a miracle," he said as they panted for breath.

"How on earth did they find you here?" asked Jeremy.

"That wonderful Red Cross," sighed Mr. Hoffman. "My mother must have guessed that I had come to America, and the Red Cross found me through the Immigration and Naturalization Service of the Department of Justice. I am registered there as an alien with a permit to stay in this country. Some day I shall become a citizen like you. And now I can hope to bring my family over here, too."

Suddenly his face fell. The joy left his eyes. They looked bleak. He groaned and sank onto a wooden painting stool.

"My dear children, I forgot! Oh, this is terrible. Terrible! I am in most dreadful trouble."

"Wh-what do you mean?" Jerry and Jenny asked in one voice.

"I cannot tell you. It is too dreadful. You will never like me again."

"Tell us," pleaded Jenny. "Maybe we can help. Please trust us!" She was eager but half afraid to have him explain.

Karl Hoffman stared at them blankly. The ruddy color drained from his cheeks. He shook his head.

Jerry drew a deep breath. In a voice that trembled he asked, "Is it anything to do with those two men who were here the day you rescued Jenny from the ledge?"

Karl Hoffman sat up straight, his face frightened. "What do you mean? What do you know?" he asked harshly.

"We really don't know anything," said Jenny. "We just suspect!"

"What do you suspect?"

Jerry answered this time. "We suspect that you are somehow mixed up in that business of stolen paintings, and that those two men have something to do with it and that they are making you do whatever you do against your will."

"Against my will," Karl Hoffman echoed, in a groan. "You two children realize that? You believe in me?"

Jenny felt a moment of guilt for ever having doubted him. "We believe in you," she said firmly.

"But how did you guess?"

"The night you came to dinner at our house, remember? There was something about the way you acted when Aunt Ruth began to talk about all those art thefts. Then Jerry began to think about the two men he saw in your studio that day he busted in on you. He had a feeling they were threatening you and

"AGAINST MY WILL"

somehow he put the two together."

"I thought no one would ever know." Karl Hoffman groaned again.

"You might just as well tell us all about it now," said Jeremy. "Maybe we can think of some way to help."

Karl Hoffman walked to the window overlooking the dam. He stood there silently for several moments, staring unseeingly at the water flowing past. When he turned around there was appeal in his eyes.

"I thank you for believing in me," he said. "I will have to trust you with the whole story." He drew a deep breath.

"Those two men, they are wicked men. They stole paintings from the house of a rich man. They intend to make him pay a ransom to get them back. They are agents of the powers that control my country and they will use the money they get by this evil means for the benefit of those who mistreat my people, who enslave them. Oh, it is monstrous that I should have to help them do this! But they told me they would make my father and mother suffer if I did not do as they said. They forced me to alter the paintings so they could not be recognized. You see, I had no choice."

"But what did you do to the paintings?" asked Jennifer.

"I disguised them. I painted a new picture on the surface of the old. The Renoir became a scene of Riverbend. The Degas, a still life of flowers. Until the ransom has been paid they hang in full view in the gallery outside in perfect security without anyone realizing that these two paintings, among the many other innocent ones, conceal stolen masterpieces."

"But suppose someone wanted to buy them?" Jerry asked.

"There is a little ticket marked 'sold' attached to the frame of each. Whoever admires them will realize they have already been spoken for."

"Then what happens?" Jenny's eyes were big.

"The ransom gets paid. The men come back and pretend they are the ones who have bought my paintings. Me, I take no money. I would not soil my hands with money from them. They deliver these paintings to the real owner, who has an expert remove with a solvent the brush strokes I have done over the original pictures. You understand? It is a very clever scheme, and such a wicked one! I have had to help against my will several times before this."

Jerry's mind had been working full speed.

"But don't you see? You won't ever have to do it again! They can't threaten you now. Your family is safe!"

Mr. Hoffman sank onto the stool, a look of wonder

"AGAINST MY WILL"

on his face. "You are right! Of course! How could I not remember that? Thank the good Lord! They cannot get at my family now!"

Abruptly he fell silent, his face more troubled than before.

"What's the matter?" Jerry and Jenny were puzzled.

"There is still a large difficulty for me," he said, speaking slowly. "I have broken the law. I have aided in theft. What will the police do to me? What will people like your parents and your Aunt Ruth think of me? Or my students, or the good people of Riverbend? My reputation will be gone. I may not be permitted to stay in this country. The authorities might send me away."

"But you can help catch the thieves!" Jerry cried. "Those men won't know that your family is safe. At least they don't know it yet. When they come to get the paintings, you can set a trap for them. If the police catch these art thieves with your help, that ought to make them go easy on you. And when they know why you did what you did, how you were forced into it to save your family and that you didn't do it for pay, I bet you won't be blamed."

Mr. Hoffman began to pace up and down. "Jeremy, what you say gives me hope. If I help the police, maybe they will not count what I did against me. And those two bad men will not be able to steal paintings any more."

"What I think we should do," said Jenny, "is to tell Daddy all about this right away. He will know what to do next."

"Jenny is right," said Mr. Hoffman. "It is too big and difficult a problem for us to handle by ourselves."

XIII

The Art Thieves

Mr. Lane looked up from his desk in surprise. He had not expected a visit from his children on Friday afternoon, much less the artist Karl Hoffman.

He pushed the papers he had been working on to one side and rose, smiling. "Hello, Karl," he said. "Good to see you. Jeremy and Jennifer, what brings you here?"

"We have *private* business to discuss with you," said Jennifer importantly.

Mr. Lane walked over to the door and closed it so they could talk unheard by a secretary and clerk in the outer office. He was amused and puzzled.

"Sit down, Karl. This chair is fairly comfortable. You kids will have to share the bench or sit on the floor. All right, spill it." He leaned back in his own swivel chair and lit his pipe.

Jenny burst out at once with the news about Mr. Hoffman's family.

"That's wonderful!" said Mr. Lane. "I'm delighted! We all realize how concerned you have been for their safety. I can't tell you how happy this news makes me." There was a pause. "But why the long faces? Is there something I can do?"

"Mr. Hoffman's in a lot of trouble," said Jeremy.

"Let's hear about it."

They took turns telling him. His face grew more and more astonished as the story unfolded. Mr. Hoffman confirmed details as they went along and explained how he had been forced into helping the art thieves.

There was a long silence after they finished. The children waited fearfully. Mr. Hoffman betrayed his nervousness by cracking his knuckles and fidgeting in his chair.

"I've been debating in my mind whether this is a matter for the FBI or the State Police," Mr. Lane said finally. "Kidnaping is a Federal offense, but picture napping is something else again. I believe the State Police can handle it. We had better call

THE ART THIEVES

them. What day do you expect your two friends?"

"*Not* my friends!" Karl Hoffman was indignant.

"Of course not! I was being ironic. I realize the spot you were in—those men holding the fate of your family over your head unless you did what they demanded. It's an old trick used many times before on the victims of dictators. I doubt if the police blame you, particularly if you help catch the thieves. Now tell me, when do you think they will come to pick up the paintings?"

"Excuse me my anger," said Karl Hoffman. "You understand! My gratitude is yours. The men, they come Sunday evening. When they know I have no class and the gallery is not open to the public."

"Good," said Mr. Lane. "Do not worry anymore. Go about your business—I mean your art—as usual. And trust me! As my children have trusted you. I did not know I had produced offshoots of Sherlock Holmes in my family."

"Sherlock Holmes? Who is he?" Mr. Hoffman was puzzled.

Jeremy chuckled. "He was a great English detective in stories by Arthur Conan Doyle. Slick stories! He deduced—just put two and two together the way we did—and always in the end came out with the right answers."

Jeremy realized he sounded smug. He reddened.

"It was an accident with us, with him it was brains!"

"Well," said Mr. Lane with a grin, "I'm glad you see the difference! Now let *me* go about my business."

Karl Hoffman got up from his chair, bowed, and said, "I deeply thank you. I leave my fate in your hands."

"So long, Dad," said Jeremy.

Jenny gave her father a quick kiss. "I feel better!" she said.

On Sunday evening when two men in a shabby sedan drove up to the Riverbend Art Center, the police were waiting for them. One state trooper was concealed inside the gallery. Others hid outside. As soon as the two men left their car and unsuspectingly entered the building, the state troopers closed in, covering every exit so there could be no escape.

The men were about to accept the paintings from Karl Hoffman's hands when a state trooper emerged from behind a door, gun in hand, and said quietly, "You are under arrest."

There was no struggle. The men were taken completely by surprise. They cursed Mr. Hoffman in his own language and told him his family would pay for this, but he laughed in their faces.

Disdaining to speak anything but English, he told them that his family was free and safe from any-

THE ART THIEVES

thing they could do to him or them and that they no longer had any hold over him.

The next day the large city papers carried front-page stories about the arrest of the art thieves and the recovery of the paintings. Reporters came to Riverbend, interviewed Karl Hoffman, took photographs of him, the Riverbend Art Center, the art gallery itself, and of the Renoir and Degas in their disguises.

MYSTERY OF THE HIDDEN FACE

Reproductions of the paintings as they looked in their original state were printed alongside. The news articles told how Hoffman had been forced into aiding the art thieves to keep his family in East Germany from suffering, and that as soon as he learned they had escaped he had gone immediately to the authorities and helped the police trap the criminals.

Overnight Karl Hoffman became a celebrity. Offers of money poured in from generous-hearted Americans to help bring his family to the United States. Others offered to help provide living quarters and jobs for his father and brother-in-law.

The wealthy Mr. Sampson who owned the paintings assured Karl Hoffman he would not prosecute him for his part in the crime and commissioned the artist to remove the overpainting from the surface of the real pictures. The owner was so glad to know that his masterpieces were safe and to have the ransom money returned he promised to use his influence to secure Karl Hoffman a position with one of the big city museums.

Jenny and Jeremy did not learn any of these details until late Tuesday afternoon when Karl Hoffman was finally free to come to see them. Aunt Ruth was with him. He told them everything that had happened since he had said good-by to them after leaving Mr. Lane's office the previous Friday afternoon. When he had finished he said, "My cup runneth over. I did not believe I could ever be so nearly happy again."

"It is good to see you like this, Karl," said Aunt Ruth. "No clouds hanging heavy over your head."

"Ruth is going to help me celebrate," said Karl Hoffman, looking at her in a way that gave Jenny pleasurable shivers. "We are going to borrow a canoe and paddle up the river to a spot I've found, and I am going to build a fire and broil her a steak in true American style."

"Won't that be fun?" said Aunt Ruth.

Jenny gave Jerry a quick glance. This sounded promising. Jerry was dense. "Can we come, too?" he asked.

Karl Hoffman looked at Aunt Ruth in an embarrassed sort of way. But before he could say anything, Mrs. Lane said a firm *no*. "You and Jenny have to baby-sit with Debby this evening. Your father and I are going out."

Karl got up from the canvas chair where he had been reclining. "Another time, my young friends to whom I owe so much, another time I will plan a cookout just for you."

Jenny nudged Jerry as Aunt Ruth and Karl opened the terrace screen door and went down the brick wall. "You dope!" she exploded. "Can't you see they want to be alone?"

Jerry was stunned. "Gosh, I *am* dumb," he said.

"Do you think he really is that way about her?"

Jenny tossed her head and half closed her eyes while her lips curled up in a wide pleased smile. "I don't know, but I sure hope," she said.

"Stop romancing," said Mrs. Lane with a laugh. "It's time to set the table for supper."

XIV

Karl Hoffman's Plan

Jenny slid *woosh* down the polished bannister in Grandmother Turner's house, landing with a thud at the foot of the stairs. It was Saturday morning following the arrest of the art thieves.

Grandfather, from the big wing chair in the living room, looked over his half-moon glasses and asked mildly, "Don't you think you've done that enough, child?"

"This is my last time," said Jennifer. "But I promised to hold Debby on while she has a turn."

"All right," said Grandfather. "You'll wear out the seat of your pants if you keep it up, but give

MYSTERY OF THE HIDDEN FACE

Debby a turn and then let this old man have a bit of quiet."

Jenny climbed the carpeted stairs, two steps at a time. She boosted Debby onto the bannister. Then holding her firmly so she wouldn't topple off, she helped her little sister slide down the long slope of shiny rail.

Debby squealed with delight. "Do it again," she pleaded.

"No, Deb, Grandpa wants to read his paper. We'll go outside now."

Jenny wished the invitation from Mother's old college friend for Mother and Dad to spend a long week end at the shore had included children. But Grandmother had said that it was nice for parents to go away by themselves sometimes. Of course it was expensive to take a family of five away for a vacation. That was why Daddy usually spent his holiday at home puttering around and doing all of the odd jobs he usually didn't have time enough for when he was at the office. It was a real treat for Mother and Dad to go away over two nights without any children or other responsibilities. The more Jenny thought about it the more she thought they deserved it, and was glad they had gone.

It was fun to be at Grandmother Turner's, especially with Aunt Ruth still there. Jenny slept in the

KARL HOFFMAN'S PLAN

other twin bed in her room and Debby in a cot at the foot of the beds. Jerry was in the little back room next to the bathroom. He especially liked that location. There was a porch roof which he could reach from his window with a tree standing handily by. He much preferred going out the window onto the roof and down the tree trunk to using the stairs. Grandfather forbade Jenny to try it and she had promised Mother to be good so she didn't dare disobey.

Karl Hoffman had taken Aunt Ruth to the movies the night before. Jenny and Debby were in bed when Aunt Ruth got home. Deb was sound asleep and Jenny pretended to be. She secretly watched Aunt Ruth as she stood in front of the dresser brushing her hair by the one shaded light. Jenny could see her aunt's reflection in the mirror. There was a glow about her as though she were very happy. As Aunt Ruth turned and came over to the bed, Jenny blinked her eyes tight shut and kept them that way while Aunt Ruth lightly kissed her. She heard her aunt slide into her own bed and snuggle down on the pillows. Jenny let her breath out in a soft sigh filled with hope and in no time was asleep.

She thought about this now as she and Debby made their way out through the French doors of the dining room and down the stone steps to the terrace. There they found Aunt Ruth stretched out on a deck chair, a novel open in her hands, but her eyes fixed in the unseeing stare of a daydreamer. Jenny was dying to ask questions about last night, but she knew that was the best way of *not* finding out what she wanted to know.

Aunt Ruth brought her attention back from wherever it had been. "What are you two up to?" she asked.

"Grandpa shooed us away from the bannister so I guess we'll go down to the brook and skip stones. Or wade," said Jenny.

"You come, too," said Debby hopping from one foot to the other, her eyes big and beseeching.

"I'm too comfortable right here," said Aunt Ruth. She stretched and yawned. "I've got a good book, too, when I can stir up enough ambition to read it."

The two girls left her and followed the flagstone path through the backyard to the rustic arbor covered with the gay trumpets of heavenly blue morning glories. As they came abreast the barn, Jerry rolled down the lane on his bike, gravel spurting out from the wheels. He braked to a stop.

"I've just been over at the mill," he said. "Karl Hoffman has a wonderful idea."

"What is it?" Jenny asked as he dismounted and propped his bike against the gray shingled walls of the barn, which was no longer used for horses but sheltered Grandpa's car.

"He said he'd like to do something for Mother and Dad to show how much he appreciates everything and he suggested that while they are away he start restoring the portrait of four-times-Great-Grandma. And he won't charge a penny for it!"

"Yoiks!" said Jenny. "That's a nifty idea. Mother has been wanting to have it repaired, but she'd never agree to letting him do it for nothing. This way she won't have anything to say about it! I suppose we have to take the painting to him?"

"Yes, he wants it right away. Even so, it won't be finished by the time they get back Sunday night. He explained that the glue would have to dry and the new paint where he does retouching. Ma will just have to put up with an empty frame for a few days. You know where Grandma keeps the key to our house? Nip in and get it. He said he'd come with us and help take the painting out of its frame. It has to be handled carefully."

Debby had gotten restless. She tugged at Jenny's hand. "Jenny and Debby go to brook," she said.

"I can't after all, Deb. I'm sorry."

"Then Debby go with you."

Jenny looked at Jeremy questioningly. He shook his head. "Deb, it wouldn't be any fun for you. We won't stay long. Come on, we'll ask Aunt Ruth if she'll read to you while we're gone. When we get back I'll take you wading. Promise."

Debby blinked back the tears that had been threatening and ran up the path. She threw herself on Aunt Ruth. "Read to me!" she demanded.

Aunt Ruth cuddled Debby to her. "Where's that magic word?"

"Please read to me!"

"When you remember your manners you are hard to resist," said Aunt Ruth with a chuckle.

"If you don't mind, we'd appreciate it, too," said Jenny. She told her aunt about Karl Hoffman's plan.

"Oh, I knew about it," said Aunt Ruth. "He told me about it last night and I encouraged him to ask you. It's the one way he can think of to repay your parents and I think he should be allowed to. He considers it small enough for what your father did for him."

"Then you won't mind taking care of Deb while we're gone. Good! Go get the book you want, Debby, and I'll get our house key."

A half hour later Jeremy and Jennifer and Karl Hoffman unlocked the door of the Lane house. It gave Jenny a funny feeling to be entering her own empty house knowing neither Mother nor Dad would be there.

KARL HOFFMAN'S PLAN

"Remember the night we came home from the picnic on the river and thought a burglar had broken in?" asked Jeremy.

"I sure do!" said Jenny. "Racky-Pooh made more mess than a dozen burglars!"

"What is this about burglars?" Mr. Hoffman asked. "Do you mean there have been other thieves beside the ones we just caught at the art center?"

Jenny laughed. "This one was quite a different sort of burglar. We came home all unsuspecting and found chairs overturned, the kitchen a shambles and . . ."

Jerry interrupted. "You should have seen Dad armed with a poker and Mother with a broom, tiptoeing upstairs looking for the thief, and then their faces when it turned out to be a raccoon eating a melon in the bedroom!"

"A raccoon! I never!" Karl Hoffman laughed too. "What did you do with it?"

"Dad threw a bedspread over it and we scooped it up and carried it outdoors. It lived in our chicken coop for a few days until it managed to unlatch the door and escape."

The air inside the house was stuffy. Jerry busied himself opening windows while Jenny continued to talk about their housebreaker.

"It took us ages to clean up the kitchen," she finished, "but if it hadn't been for Racky-Pooh we would never have found out we were missing heirs." She stopped in dismay. "I forgot! I'm not supposed to talk about that to anyone outside the family."

"Then you mustn't," said Karl Hoffman.

She gave him a long, searching look, then blurted out, "But we hope you are going to be *in* the family!" and at once turned bright pink at the enormity of what she had just said.

Slow color rose in Karl's cheeks. "You mean," he asked, "you mean you think I might have a chance with your Aunt Ruth? And you wouldn't mind?"

Jenny gave a skip of delight. *She'd been right all along!* "Mind! We'd be tickled to death! And I think Aunt Ruth would be, too." She hastened to add, "Not that I know for sure, you understand, or that she's said anything. All I mean is I think you have a good chance and Jerry and I would love to have you for an uncle!"

Karl Hoffman stooped down and gathered Jenny up in a bear hug. She hugged him back, her heart singing. They both had completely forgotten her slip about the missing heir. "Let us keep this to ourselves," whispered Mr. Hoffman as Jeremy came to join them. Jerry sensed something but for once was tactful enough not to pry.

"Come on," he said. "I've put the step-stool from the kitchen next to the sideboard so Mr. Hoffman can

KARL HOFFMAN'S PLAN

get the portrait down."

Phoebe King Lane eyed them sternly as they entered the dining room. Sunlight pouring through the wide dining room window illumined the white lace frill of her bonnet and touched her lined cheeks with a warm glow.

"She's not going to like this," Jenny spoke softly.

"Baloney!" said Jeremy. "Don't go imagining things."

"Who knows, she may appreciate having her face lifted," said Karl Hoffman.

He stepped up on the stool, leaned toward the heavy mahogany frame, and gently removed it from the hook on the wall. Then, holding the frame in both hands, he returned to the floor. In the strong daylight the crack in the painting was very noticeable.

"When I have glued the crack together and filled in all of those bare areas where the paint has flaked off and cleaned the painting, your many-times-great-grandma won't know herself!" Karl Hoffman dusted off his hands. He turned the painting around. The painted panel was held inside the frame with little wedges of wood.

"Do you have a screwdriver handy?" he asked, turning to Jeremy. "I'll need something like that to pry these bits of wood loose in order to take the portrait out of the frame."

KARL HOFFMAN'S PLAN

Jerry went to the kitchen and returned with a small screwdriver from the drawer where Mother kept household tools.

One by one Karl Hoffman removed the small wood wedges. He pressed his fingers against the face of the portrait and as soon as the last wedge was loose from the frame he lifted the wooden panel out.

"What have we here?" he exclaimed. "The entire panel seems to be split into two layers." As he spoke the rear layer fell back, leaving a very thin, cracked panel of wood bearing four-times-Great-Grandmother Lane's portrait in Mr. Hoffman's hands.

Jenny and Jerry's mouths flew open. To their utter amazement they saw, face up on the floor, another painting—the portrait of a young girl.

XV

Great-Grandmother's Secret

For a moment they were speechless.

Jenny recovered first. "Who can she be?" she asked. They stared at the second portrait. A girl with a proud nose and far-apart hazel eyes looked up at them from the past. She had a wide mouth with a full underlip. Her glossy chestnut hair was parted in the middle above a rounded forehead and brushed smoothly down to her ears where it was tied into clusters of long curls. She wore a rose-sprigged cotton gown, square of neck, with puffed sleeves. Her hands were folded demurely below her softly curved bodice. The colors in the painting were clear and unstained by time.

"She is lovely, whoever she is," said Karl Hoffman. "I would say offhand she had been painted by a good artist. But why would your ancestor choose to cover up such a young and lovely face with her own?"

"Maybe this will tell us something," said Jeremy. He stooped and retrieved several thin sheets of paper that had up to now gone unnoticed. They were covered with spidery handwriting and had apparently fluttered to the floor from between the two panels of wood. It was a letter and began: "My beloved daughter, Melissa."

GREAT-GRANDMOTHER'S SECRET

"Melissa!" Jenny shouted. "Do you s'pose it's her? I mean she?"

"Who is Melissa?" asked Karl.

"She was the daughter of our four-times-great-grandma. She died young and left a little baby boy. He was our great-great-grandfather and if we could only prove he was her son but that he was adopted by his Uncle Charles, we could prove we *are* the missing heirs!"

"Jenny! Hush! Don't spill the beans," Jerry cautioned. "Remember what Dad said."

"I'm *not* spilling any beans! Mr. Hoffman is going to *be* family! Oh!" she looked crestfallen. "I guess I have spilled some after all! But never mind that now. All I can think of is Melissa. Oh, how I hope this letter is the proof we need!"

Karl Hoffman threw up his hands. "I am lost," he said. "I don't know what this is all about. Missing heirs. Spilled beans! Great-great-grandfathers. It is—how do you say—an enigma, a puzzle!"

"It sure is a puzzle," Jerry agreed.

"Well, why do we not read the letter?" asked Mr. Hoffman. "Maybe then the puzzle will be explained."

Jerry handed the sheets of paper to Jenny. "You read it, Jen, if you can make out those hen scratches."

Jenny's hands trembled as she took the letter. "I'll try," she said. She began haltingly. The handwriting

MYSTERY OF THE HIDDEN FACE

was slanted and flowed evenly. The letters were faded but well formed. The letter *s* was written as though it was an *f*. This confused Jenny at first. She read slowly, stumbling over some big words she didn't know. This is what the letter said.

MY BELOVED DAUGHTER MELISSA:

My heart breaks as I address you thus, for you were my beloved daughter though you will never know it now. Unless—in that after life where you have gone you will somehow be aware that your mother mourns you and desires your forgiveness.

Oh, if you could know the secret tears that I have shed, the chastisement I have given my own soul—for pride, for willfulness, for hardness of heart.

You were my joy, the only one of my girl children to reach maturity. I had fastened so many hopes on you. With your beauty, grace, and fine intelligence I wanted you to have a good and gracious life and to be married to a man worthy of you.

Instead, you broke my heart. You ran away with that good-for-nothing Calvert. Oh, I know he was charming. Anyone who looked like Bancroft and had his manners could turn a girl's head. But I had hoped I had instilled in you a yardstick to judge character and an appreciation of the importance of integrity, to help you detect the real from the false.

Alas, my child, you found out for yourself—the hard way. Your Bancroft Calvert turned out to be as worthless and undependable, if not downright dis-

GREAT-GRANDMOTHER'S SECRET

honest, as I feared. He was the black sheep of a fine family, as much to be trusted as quicksilver. What good did his family's position and wealth do you? They cast Bancroft off, ignored you. When he could no longer tie himself down to a sickly wife and a baby, you dared not appeal to them. It is my constant grief that you refused to turn to me, your mother. I understand, though, that you had too much of the King pride to ask anything of a mother who had cut you off.

Instead, after you learned your husband had been killed in a duel, you wrote your brother Charles. He came as you lay dying. Charles held your hand and promised you to bring your son up as his own. When breath had gone he closed your eyes and brought your body home for burial. He gave his name to your boy. This grandchild of mine I cannot tolerate around me. In him I see you whom I loved and lost. Your face in this painting is a constant invitation to remorse. I can no longer bear to look on it. Now I have had my own likeness painted. I cannot destroy yours. But mine will cover it in the same frame. And when my own stern eyes look out at me, they will condemn me for what I am.

In my right mind, and with an aching heart, I sign this now, on the 20th day of September, 1842, never expecting that it will be read.

PHOEBE KING LANE

Tears glistened in Jenny's eyes when she had finished. Jerry cleared his throat and Mr. Hoffman coughed. Here was a close-up of tragedy that they had not expected.

"Poor Phoebe Lane and poor Melissa!" sighed Jenny. "How they both must have suffered. They never seemed very real to me before."

"To me either," said Jerry. "But now I understand why there was a line drawn through Melissa's name in the family Bible. Her mother must have done it."

"Poor girl," said Karl, "to die so young."

The information contained in the letter had been slowly percolating in Jerry's mind. "Say!" he exclaimed. "Do you see what this letter means, Jen? It's the proof-positive Dad has a right to the money as the missing heir!"

He looked at Karl. "We'll have to let you in on this now. Will you keep mum?"

"Whatever you tell me in confidence will go no farther," he assured them. "If you would rather not tell me, I'll understand."

"No," said Jerry. "After hearing this much I think you ought to know the rest. Don't you, Jen?"

There was no doubt in Jenny's mind. So they told him about accidentally finding their father's middle name in the listing by Tracers Company of America in an old newspaper the night the raccoon broke into the house, and thereby discovering they had a possible claim to the forgotten fortune of Robert Bancroft

GREAT-GRANDMOTHER'S SECRET

Calvert. "The only trouble is we can't prove it," said Jerry. "We found out that Robert Bancroft Calvert was a first cousin of Dad's great-grandfather whose mother was Melissa. But we couldn't find any record of that great-grandfather's adoption by his uncle Charles Lane, or that his name had been switched around so that Calvert was his middle name instead of his last name."

"Then some other distant Calverts turned up," said Jenny. "They weren't as close kin as we thought we were, but they had real proof of their family connection, and we didn't. So you see how important this letter is."

"Wow!" Jerry couldn't contain himself. "Our dad is going to whoop for joy when he sees it. He'd given up hope that there was any chance for us."

"I could whoop myself!" exclaimed Karl. "I did not dream this plan of mine to restore the portrait would have a result like this!"

"Shall we call Mother and Dad and tell them to come home?" asked Jenny.

"That would be too bad," said Karl. "They are having a nice vacation and good news will keep. Nothing can be done until after Sunday anyway. Let your mother and father come home and discover Melissa in the frame on the dining room wall. Then you will have this other happy surprise for them."

MYSTERY OF THE HIDDEN FACE

He skillfully fitted the portrait of Melissa into the wide frame and wedged it tight. Then he remounted the stool steps and hung it on the wall. The proud young face looked down on them, serene and ageless.

"She has withstood the years so well because her portrait has been sealed from dust and air by her mother's face," Karl explained. He picked up the painting of Phoebe King Lane. "I will take this to my studio and start work on her at once. Jenny, find a safe place in your father's desk and put the letter there."

Jenny ran to do so. She took a manila folder from a tall pigeonhole and placed the letter inside. As they left the house she said, "I was certain all the time that four-times-Great-Grandma had a secret if we could only make her tell us!"

… XVI …

Spilled Beans

When Mr. and Mrs. Lane drove into the driveway at Grandmother Turner's late Sunday afternoon they found their three children sitting on the porch steps waiting for them. There were excited greetings, hugs and kisses, and exclamations about what a good time Mr. and Mrs. Lane had had.

"Where are Grandma and Grandpa?" asked their mother, looking around. It was unlike them not to be on hand to welcome her.

"They're at our house," said Jenny. "Grammy and Aunt Ruth have fixed a picnic supper for all of us there on the terrace."

"The dears!" said Mrs. Lane.

"Let's get going," said their dad.

Jenny was busting to tell about the surprise at home. She jigged up and down with impatience as Jerry stowed their bags in the car. Then he and Debby and Jenny piled in.

Mr. Lane backed out of the driveway, crossed over the bridge spanning Beaver Brook, and turned left on Main Street past the Sunday silence of the stores and business buildings. They rattled over the long river bridge, drove by Riverbend House, and turned into their own lane where their Dad stopped the car.

"Don't bother with suitcases," said Jenny. "Come into the house right away. We have a surprise for you!"

Debby was already scrambling up the porch steps. Grandma opened the screen door.

"Come on into the dining room," urged Jenny, hardly giving her mother time to kiss Grammy and Grandpa.

Aunt Ruth and Karl Hoffman were waiting there and at first Mr. and Mrs. Lane were so busy saying hello to them they didn't notice anything different about the room. In the late afternoon the sun did not pour through the wide window as it did in the morning to illumine the portrait. Jenny remedied that. She

SPILLED BEANS

turned on the lights. "Look!" she cried, gesturing toward the wall.

"Wh-wh-why?" stuttered Mrs. Lane, "where did four-times-Great-Grandma go? Who is that?"

"She's Melissa!" Jerry and Jenny shouted.

"Melissa!" echoed Mr. Lane. The lovely young face ignored his astonished gaze.

"But what? Why? How did she get here?"

"Let Mr. Hoffman tell," said Jerry.

Karl looked at Jenny questioningly. She nodded. "Well, it was like this," he said. "I remembered your wish some day to have the portrait of the ancestor restored—the crack mended and the painting cleaned and so forth—and I thought to myself this was a good time, while you are off on a holiday. I had a great wish in my heart to do something for you that would please you and would help me to say thank you for for what you have done for me." He stopped and looked at Mr. Lane helplessly. "I am not good at saying what I mean, but I hope you understand. That is why I suggested to Jeremy that we remove the grandmother from the frame and I take her to my studio so I could have the work begun before you returned. When we took the panel from the frame yesterday, it separated into two panels—this one of the daughter concealed beneath the portrait of her mother."

"Well, I'll be!" exclaimed Mr. Lane. "Why would

MYSTERY OF THE HIDDEN FACE

she do a thing like that?"

"You'll simply pop when you know," cried Jenny. She ran to get the letter from her father's desk. "Read this!" she said. "It fell out from between the two portraits."

Dazedly Mr. Lane spread out the fragile old sheets of paper on the dining room table.

"Read it aloud," begged Mrs. Lane. "We all want to hear."

And so, while the others heard for the first time, Jenny and Jerry and Mr. Hoffman heard once again the tragic story of a headstrong girl and a mother's self-reproach.

Mr. Lane read with mounting excitement as the import of the letter dawned on him. When he came to the part about Melissa's brother Charles giving his name to her baby boy, he stopped briefly and said, "Dorothy you realize that this is the proof we needed?"

Mrs. Lane nodded, her eyes bright.

It is odd to feel at once sad and happy, Jenny thought. *Sad because what happened to Melissa and her mother was so sad, but happy because of what this letter would mean to us, their descendants.*

When Mr. Lane finally finished in a voice he was having some difficulty in controlling, it was as though a spell had been cast on everyone in the room. Melissa's

SPILLED BEANS

ageless young face regarded them distantly and serenely across the years.

Grandpa Turner took out a snowy handkerchief and blew his nose loudly. The sound released them from the spell.

"I don't know which one I feel sorriest for," said Grandma, with a little gulp.

"I don't really feel sorry for Melissa," said Aunt Ruth slowly. "She did what she wanted to do, regardless of consequences, and she paid for her headstrongness. Her mother had to live with a broken heart all those long years after."

Mr. Lane smoothed the letter carefully and returned it to the manila folder. "I understand now why my Grandfather Jonathan wasn't enthusiastic about his Great-Grandmother Phoebe and kept her portrait in the attic. He must have inherited the portrait from his father for whom I was named, Henry Calvert Lane. I suspect Henry at some time mentioned that his grandmother could not stand the sight of him and Jonathan—my grandfather—undoubtedly resented it. I can almost hear him say, 'Well, then, I can't stand the sight of her, either,' and when the portrait became his, he consigned it to the attic. I'll have to check their dates again, but Phoebe lived to be ninety-four so I expect she was still around when my grandfather was born."

He looked at the portrait of Melissa. "I myself am very grateful to Phoebe King Lane for writing this letter and hiding it as she did. At the time she wrote it she could never have foreseen how much these sheets of paper would mean to her great-great-great-grandson. I'm going to take them myself to the bank in Philadelphia tomorrow. I won't trust them to the mail. There's no question in my mind that the information in this letter will prove my claim to the forgotten fortune of Robert Bancroft Calvert."

Jenny danced around the table singing, "Dad's the missing heir, Dad's the missing heir, Heigh-ho the derryo, Dad's the missing heir!"

"Da-da not missing. Da-da here!" Debby said.

Everyone laughed.

"You knew about this?" Mr. Lane asked Karl Hoffman.

"Yes," he said. "When Jenny read the letter aloud to Jeremy and me she couldn't help—how do you say?—spill the beans!"

"No, I couldn't," said Jenny. "I didn't think it mattered since he's practically *in* the family."

Aunt Ruth's face flushed a most lovely color. She looked at Karl. He gave her a wide warm smile. "May I tell them?" he asked. "Though this time it is *my* beans Jennifer is spilling."

"Tell, tell!" begged Debby.

SPILLED BEANS

"I am going to be your Uncle Karl someday, Debby. Your Aunt Ruth has consented to marry me."

"Hallelujah!" shouted Jenny, beside herself with delight. Mrs. Lane hugged her sister and Mr. Lane pumped Karl Hoffman's hand. Grandma and Grandpa looked pleased but not at all surprised, for they had already been let in on the secret.

"When is the wedding?" asked Jenny when she could make herself heard.

"It's all been so sudden we haven't decided yet," said Aunt Ruth. "But I'm counting on having you for a junior bridesmaid, Jenny, and Debby will be my flower girl."

"Oh, Aunt Ruth!" Jenny was starry-eyed. Debby gave a squeal of delight, guessing this must be something special.

The picnic party on the terrace became a very merry party, indeed. Grandma had provided mounds of delicious sandwiches. There were bowls of red-ripe sliced tomatoes and carrot sticks and olives. There were tall glasses of iced tea and lemonade and milk, and a plate of cookies.

Aunt Ruth sparkled and shone. Karl Hoffman glowed with pride and happiness. Grandma and Grandpa radiated satisfaction. Jenny and Jerry ate their fill and basked in the sunshine of everybody's smiles.

Jenny feasted her inner eye on the entrancing vision of Aunt Ruth gowned in bridal white and herself floating down the aisle in a heavenly-blue morning-glory dress ahead of the bride, with Debby strewing rose petals before them. In the midst of these pleasant imaginings she was struck with a sudden question.

"Where are we going to put four-times-Great-Grandma when Uncle Karl"—she gave him a mischievous glance—"has her all restored?"

"*Not* back in the attic," said Mother. "I am going to hunt and hunt until I find another antique mahogany frame like the one that frames Melissa, and then I'm going to place them side by side. I think it would please Great Grandma."

"I do, too," said Jenny.